PENGUII

MARINE

MARK CHIUSANO is a graduate of Harvard University, where he was the recipient of a Hoopes Prize for outstanding undergraduate fiction. His stories have appeared in *Guernica, Narrative, Harvard Review*, and online at *Tin House* and *The Paris Review Daily*. He was born and raised in Brooklyn.

Praise for Mark Chiusano's
Marine Park: Stories

"In clean, honed prose, Mark Chiusano gives us an intimate tour of a neighborhood of Brooklyn not offered up in fiction before. His explorations of loyalty within a family, and the breach of it, are startling and affecting—his sense of story is impeccable. *Marine Park* is a debut worth a reader's close attention."

—Amy Hempel, author of *The Collected Stories of Amy Hempel*

"The stories in *Marine Park* are funny and touching and elliptical, and all about coming of age at the edge of the city and on the margins of the good life, with some moving forward and others left behind. Mark Chiusano is wonderful on how our minds can be elsewhere even when we wish to be wholly present, and on the oblique ways in which we therefore often have to signal our indispensability to one another."

—Jim Shepard, author of *You Think That's Bad*

MARINE PARK

Stories

MARK CHIUSANO

PENGUIN BOOKS

PENGUIN BOOKS
Published by the Penguin Group
Penguin Group (USA) LLC
375 Hudson Street
New York, New York 10014

USA | Canada | UK | Ireland | Australia
New Zealand | India | South Africa | China
penguin.com
A Penguin Random House Company

First published in Penguin Books 2014

The following magazines published earlier versions of several stories in this collection: *The Bad Version* ("Vampire Deer on Jekyll Island"), *Blip* ("Why Don't You"), *The Harvard Advocate* ("Air-Conditioning," "Car Parked on Quentin, Being Washed," and "We Were Supposed"), *The Harvard Crimson* ("The Tree"), *Harvard Review* ("To Live in the Present Moment Is a Miracle"), *Narrative* ("Heavy Lifting"), and *The Utopian* ("Shatter the Trees and Blow Them Away").

LIBRARY OF CONGRESS CATALOGING-IN-PUBLICATION DATA
Chiusano, Mark.
Marine Park : stories / Mark Chiusano.
pages cm
ISBN 978-0-14-312460-3
1. Marine Park (New York, N.Y.)—Fiction.   I. Title.
PS3603.H5745M37   2014
813'.6—dc23
2014006051

Printed in the United States of America
1 3 5 7 9 10 8 6 4 2

Set in Adobe Caslon Pro   Designed by Elke Sigal

For my mother and father, and for Scott

CONTENTS

CONTENTS

MARINE PARK

HEAVY LIFTING

orris turned the key in the garage door lock, and I pulled the door up. Look, said Lorris. Icicles, he said. They were hanging from the metal runner on the bottom.

There were three shovels in the back of the garage and Lorris picked two, grasping each at its center to test the weight. He handed me the longer one, the slightly heavier one, for breaking up ice patches. He was too small for that. Then we closed the garage door.

Outside, on Avenue R, the snowdrifts went up as high as the information boxes on the bus stop poles. The fire hydrants were completely buried. We tried to put our boots in the few footsteps in the middle of the street. If we dug down we'd be walking on the double yellow line. The plows weren't out this early. I carried the shovel on my shoulder, blade up. Lorris dragged his behind him. Every once in a while he'd pick it up to knock off the snow sticking to the end.

At the first house, Lorris waited at the bottom of the stairs. You go, he said. I took off my glove to ring the bell. Shovel your walk? I asked the old woman who answered. Kenneth, she yelled behind her, before she disappeared into the warmth. A man appeared in his undershirt. Move along now, he said.

We only went to houses with driveways, for the possibility of extra work. Ones with cars in front, to say that someone was home. Often the windows with no Christmas decorations, because non-Christians paid better for this kind of thing. The rest of them shoveled little pathways down their own steps on the way to mass. Lorris was good at spotting mezuzahs nailed to the wooden frames.

At the third house a little girl answered the door. She was even younger than Lorris. She still had her pajamas on. Is your mom home? I said. Lorris looked up from the bottom of the stairs. A beautiful lady came up behind the girl, wrapped in a wool blanket. Is something wrong? she asked. Do you need some shoveling? I said. I pointed at my shovel with my bare hand.

The lady looked behind her, into the house. What're you charging? she said.

Twenty bucks, I answered. I could hear Lorris suck in his breath.

I'll give you ten, she said.

I need fifteen, I told her. She played with the hair on top of the girl's head. Clean our driveway out too? she asked.

We were always good shovelers, Lorris and I. I think we came out of the womb doing it. Lorris used the small one for finesse work—the stairs, the edges under railings, the wheel paths of cars. He did the salt, if people had it for us, though he made me carry the bags from their doorsteps to strategic central locations. I didn't like my gloves getting blue from the chemicals. I was the heavy lifting man, could carry three times my shovel's maximum load.

At the corner of Quentin, off Marine Park, a Jeep was stuck in the crosswalk. There were other crews of kids carrying their shovels on their shoulders. A big-chested man rolled down the passenger-side window and shouted into the cold: Twenty-five bucks if you get us moving. Two crews raced across the street to get there first, and because they made it at the same time, they both just started digging. A couple of early drinkers came out of the Mariners Inn without coats on, trailing steam behind them, to watch. Lorris pulled on my sleeve and said, I think Red Jacket's the best. We leaned on our shovels while the Jeep's wheels spun and shrieked, the gray slush shooting up into the shovelers' faces. One kid was jamming the shovel blade right into the rubber of the tire, and the passenger-side window rolled down again, and the man said, Hey, knock that off.

Once the Jeep lurched forward a little, a twenty-dollar bill came flying out the window and landed in the snow. Two kids dove on top of it. One of them had a Hurricanes football sweatshirt on. On the back it said, GIVE 'EM HELL. The Jeep screamed away, toward Avenue U and the Belt Parkway. Come on, Lorris, I said.

It was twelve o'clock when we finished our usual streets. Someone with a snowplow was revving his engine on Thirty-Sixth, ruining our business. A group of three men, in heavy blue sweat-shirts, jogged by us with shovels. The one in the front had hair on his face. 'Ta boys, he said. Can we go home now? Lorris whined, hitting my back with his shovel handle. Almost, I said. He un-wrapped the Rice Krispies bar he kept in his pocket for emer-gencies.

The house didn't have a doorbell. You could have told that even before you were on the stoop. Part of the front window had card-board over it. Come inside, the man said when he opened the door. We're not supposed to, Lorris called from the bottom of the un-shoveled stairs. Shut up, I told him. He followed my boot prints up.

Get the snow off your feet, the man said. I don't want water bugs in my house, he said. We stamped our feet on the rubber mat. We followed his wide back through the dark, into the kitchen. Here, he said, and put two mugs in our hands.

We sat at the kitchen table. Lorris looked at the man, and the man glowered down at him. His chest was sweaty and his firehouse T-shirt stuck to it, bleeding black through the blue. His crucifix chain hung over his shirt. I need you to do my backyard, he said.

Out the screen door, we surveyed the job. Deep, thick drifts, nowhere for good foot purchase. Fences too high to throw the snow over. A hundred dollars for the whole thing, he said.

We waded into the middle. Lorris and I started back to back. The man had put a windbreaker on and was sitting in a foldout chair with his feet up, watching us. That's it, he said. That's right. Our shovels hit the ground. We pushed off from each other, Lorris shoveling his snow to my side, where I snared it and tossed it off under the high porch. That's it, the man said.

It got so hot that we took off our jackets. The sun was higher and higher. The sweat was dripping from the blue beanies our mother made us wear. When I looked up at the man sitting there his mouth was slightly open, like he was waiting for something to happen, like he didn't think that we would finish. But we got all the snow off. We shoveled that yard until just the bare garden was showing beneath it, the soil hard as concrete that when we reached made our shovels ring.

AIR-CONDITIONING

For a while there was only one air conditioner in our house. It was in the living room, and we put it on during birthdays or the Fourth of July. It covered the heat in the kitchen from my mother burning things, like the half-sausages, the hot ones, which had a black crust on the bottom from where they touched the pan for too long.

Lorris slept in my room during the summer, even though he had his own room, because mine had a ceiling fan. It had wooden slats with small holes at the edges so that in the winter we could hang our model planes and cars off the ends. After our mother had dusted the top of the slats, we would set the fan going on a low frequency and the planes and race cars would spin around, getting higher and higher with the centripetal acceleration, until the Lego ones started to break apart and Lorris ran shouting from the room.

Our parents had been arguing in the living room, with the air conditioner masking the noise a little, and we were building Lego cars in my room, when finally I came and sat on the stairs and started reading a poem I'd written the week before about how cold the pancakes were that morning.

The pancakes, I said, were cold this morning. I was sitting with my knees together on the top step and Lorris was lying on his stomach clutching the two-by-two Lego piece I had asked him to find. I started over: The pancakes were cold this morning.

That's enough of that, said my father.

I'm just trying to help, I said.

Jamison's just trying to help, said Lorris.

It's none of your *business*, my father said. This is an adult *conversation*. From downstairs we could hear the kitchen cabinets being slammed shut. *Conversation*, he repeated.

One day my father came home carrying a second air conditioner. He was carrying it the way you carry birthday presents, as if someone was about to stack more boxes on top. He had to put the air conditioner down to ring the doorbell, even though Lorris and I had seen him through the upstairs window, and our mother went to answer it, us behind her, her shoulder and neck cradling the portable phone. She put a hand over the receiver to say, I don't even want to know.

My father was a driving instructor. He worked at the place on Kings Highway under the train tracks, where the storefronts grow on top of each other until one of them covers the other. The office for the Kings Highway Driving School was on the second floor, and they were ignoring Department of Health requests to make it handicap accessible. They posted a sign that said, FOR HANDI-CAPPED, PLEASE CALL UP. WILL COME DOWN AND GET YOU. So far they'd never had to do it.

I was thirteen at the time, and taking any seconds in the car I could get. Technically I was too young, but if we went in the practice car and lit up the sign on top that said STUDENT DRIVER, no one said anything. Everyone in our neighborhood was a cop, and they knew me and my father pretty well, so we always drove out toward the sanitation plant on Gerritsen, the shit factory, where you could make the widest turns. Sometimes we let Lorris in the back, because he always begged to come, and he took his favorite Hot Wheel, the red one with the white stripe down the middle. It was always the fastest on our yellow racetrack. He held it in both hands, mimicking the turns and motions I made while I drove.

My mother didn't like the idea of me driving, especially with my father, because she said that someday we would get caught and it would go on my permanent transcript. That was the kind of thing she was always ragging about, things on my permanent school transcript. Even though I was about to graduate, and Madison doesn't turn people away. She thought that those kinds of things ride on your bumper forever, and maybe they do, but I try to ask as few questions as possible. She wasn't around when we drove anyway, because she worked eight to six as a school secretary.

My father lounged around most mornings, doing his shifts in the office three days a week, but other than that he stayed at home until four, when the first lessons were usually scheduled. Sometimes he'd paint the basement just for something to do, or sweep the stoop. I got off the cheese bus from school around three, which left almost an hour for driving. Some days, if Lorris was late at an after-school program, we'd go pick him up. Our mother liked that the least. How could we explain ourselves picking a nine-year-old kid up at school and say this is still a lesson? She was mainly just unhappy because she thought our father wasn't a good driver, and that it was terrifying that he was teaching the whole borough below Fulton Street. Technically she might have been better, but he was confident about it, and didn't worry about hitting the brakes too hard or conserving gas. She was always stopping at yellows.

When he brought the second air conditioner home it was April, but one of those hot Aprils that remind you what summer's like, before it rains again. In Brooklyn we waited for thunderstorms. Once our father left for work and before our mother got home, I'd get the key for the garage and open the heavy door slowly, hand over hand. Lorris would be drumming on the metal as it went up. We'd pull our bikes out, his fire-yellow, mine blue and white, and race down the side streets to Marine Park by the water. There were trees on the outside of the park, basketball courts near the street. In the middle, a wide paved oval studded by baseball fields, their backstops open, facing each other across the grass. At that point in the afternoon you could feel the heat through the handlebars. We'd make it one lap around the oval, 0.84 miles, before we heard the first thunder, and then Lorris would yell and dart ahead even though he'd just gotten his training wheels off. The rain came down all at once then, and all of a sudden it would be cold, and this was the best part, when I pulled over by the water fountain and Lorris circled back to me. I pulled the two red and blue windbreakers out of my bike basket and we put them on, invincible. We rode two more laps in the storm until racing each other home.

Dad put the second air conditioner in his and Mom's room. It was just the bathroom and a closet between their room and mine, and if we had the fan on low Lorris and I could hear the air conditioner clearing its throat all night. That's what it sounded like—like it was constantly hacking something up from deep down in its throat. Sometimes if I was awake after going to the bathroom in the early a.m., I could hear our mother wake up and walk over to it, and turn it down a few settings. It took them a long time to get the hang of how high they wanted it to be. It would be too warm when they went to bed, but then freezing by morning, unless Mom got up to fix it. We could tell when she hadn't gotten up, because when we went in before school to say good-bye to Dad, on the days he was sleeping there, he'd have the white sheets all wrapped around his head from the middle of the night.

A few weeks after we got the second air conditioner it was so hot they started putting out weather advisories over 1010 WINS in the morning. Stay inside unless absolutely necessary. Mom took this to heart, and tried to get Lorris and me to do it too, though we didn't. School was winding down, especially for eighth-graders, so we didn't have homework anymore, even from Regents math. My math teacher, Mr. Pebson, had taken to sitting in the back of the classroom and spraying Lysol at anyone if they sneezed too close to him. This was in independent math, where we worked at our own pace. We took the tests when we got to the ends of chapters. At this point, everyone seemed to still have a few pages before being ready for their tests. Mr. Pebson didn't mind. He was concentrating on staying ahead of the sickness wave that always happened the first time the weather changed like this.

It got so hot that the cheese buses broke down, and we had to walk home from school. Dad would have picked us up if we told him, and he did pick Lorris up, but I convinced him that we'd gotten some special buses shipped in from upstate, where the kids biked to school all the time because it was so safe. My friend Hayden and I walked toward our neighborhood together, taking everything in.

One of those days, Hayden told me that I couldn't walk straight. I told him he was being ridiculous but it turned out he was right. I'd step with my left foot and fall two or three inches off my forward motion, and then readjust with my right foot, but four or five inches too far. Then I'd have to fix it with my left, but that came off the line a little too. I didn't know it was happening. Somehow I got wherever I was going, but Hayden showed me how, if he was standing pretty close to my shoulder, I kept knocking him, on every third or fourth step.

We were walking down Thirty-Third, which comes off Kings Highway at a curve, and suddenly I wasn't sure I'd be able to make it all the way home. The more I thought about my feet the more inches I diverged right and left. Hayden held my right arm and tried to force me forward, but I started breathing heavy and told him I needed a break. That's when the station wagon pulled over, and someone rolled down the window.

It was a high school kid, with a Madison football sweatshirt and the chinstrap beard that everyone who could was wearing that year. Hayden was pretending that the white tuft on his chin counted. The driver also had a Madison sweatshirt on, and I saw him use his right hand to put the car into park.

Don't you live on Quentin? the guy in the passenger seat said to us. You coming down from Hudde?

Hayden said yes.

Jump in, he said. We'll drop you off—it's too hot to walk. He leaned his arm out the window and reached behind to open the back door.

Once we were in the car the Madison kid in the passenger seat turned the music up, and it wasn't that it was louder than in our car but it was thumping more in my chest. You like Z100? he said, smiling, leaning his left hand behind the headrest.

I was watching the driver while Hayden answered for us. He was driving with two fingers, his index and middle ones on one hand, his other arm out the window. Somehow we were going just as fast as my dad always goes on side streets, but we were getting the soft stops that only my mom, at fifteen miles per hour, was able to get. At the stop sign on Avenue P, he jolted out to look twice, in exact time with the music. His friend was drumming on the dashboard with both hands.

Dad was sitting on the stoop when they dropped us off, and

he stood up once he recognized me getting out of the car. The car waved away. I was able to walk again, the zigzag curse gone. Hayden said, Hi, Mr. Favero, and then turned to me. That car was disgusting, huh? he said. I was looking at my dad's face. When I got up to him, he grabbed me under the armpit and dragged me up the stoop. Hayden didn't look away. We were inside with the air-conditioning on when he flat-palmed me in the stomach.

Are you serious? he said. Are you serious?

When Dad came home with the third air conditioner, it was still blistering out. There were tornadoes in Texas, more than they'd ever seen before, and in earth science Ms. Donatelli said it was what we had to look forward to: global warming in America. Someone in the back asked if this meant no more snow days, and she said, Maybe no snow, period.

He had the air conditioner in the trunk of the driving instructor car. You don't notice until you're close to it, but those cars are a little skinnier than regular ones. Dad says it helps the kids who have a bad sense of hand-eye coordination. There's more wiggle room when you're trying to squeeze through tight spaces. He says that the first thing he asks a student when they get in the car is whether they played sports when they were younger, or if they still do now. If not, he'd know it was going to be a long day. You can't imagine how crappy those kids are, especially the Hasidic Jews.

Why's that, Daddy? asked Lorris.

Because they didn't play sports as a kid, he answered, wiping his mouth with his napkin. I had set the table, and we used the white ones with blue borders that I liked.

This is how you raise your kids, Mom said. She was twirling her fork in her fingers. She'd gotten home late and he was back early.

My kids, yeah? He shrugged. It's just true.

The new air conditioner was bigger than the others, mostly because it had extendable plastic wings on the side that were supposed to be for fitting in a window. That afternoon before Mom got back from work, he put it in the kitchen, balancing it above the heater and extending the wings so it sat snug. He got some blocks of wood out of the garage and pushed them underneath.

When she came back she had immediate problems. They had a session up in their bedroom where we couldn't really hear what they were yelling. When they came down, she was pointing at the kitchen window. How am I supposed to hang the clothes out now? she said. I guess Dad hadn't thought about that. The clothesline comes out the kitchen window. He moved it one window over.

That was the spring of people breaking their wrists. I had three friends who did, and at least two more from school. Everyone was walking around with casts on their arms and permanent markers in their back pockets to ask you to sign. It happened to our next-door neighbor first—he was playing basketball at the courts by Marine Park, and when he went up for a rebound someone kneed him the wrong way. He fell full on his knuckles. I wasn't there, but Lorris had been riding his bike and said he saw him waiting for the ambulance, his hand doubled over and fingers touching forearm.

The one wrist I did get to see was right by our house. Behind the house there's an alley for the sanitation trucks to get the garbage. This way they don't clog up the avenues in the mornings. Hayden was over and Dad was showing Lorris how to skateboard. The alley has a little hill on each end and dips down in the middle. Dad had him getting speed down the hill and then showed him how to glide. Hayden and I were on our Razor scooters, trying to do grind tricks off the concrete sides of the alley. Then, after Lorris beat his own glide record and Dad was giving him a high five, Hayden decided to come down the hill backward.

Dad wasn't watching. He was pretending to shadowbox with Lorris, who was saying, I'm the greatest, I'm the greatest.

Don't do it, man, I said. They don't even try that on Tony Hawk.

It's gonna be sick, he said, and gave it a little hop to get his speed up.

He made it all the way down before falling. I have to give him credit for that. But then he swerved toward the wall and got scared and fell. He wasn't even going that fast. All I heard was a squelch, like the sound the black dried-up shark eggs make when we squish them on the beach at Coney Island. It was the same sound. His wrist looked bent sideways. He jumped up and was screaming, My wrist, my wrist, and my dad came running over, Lorris right behind, and that's when the third air conditioner fell out the window, crashing and breaking into pieces, and my mom yelling from the kitchen, Goddamnit you're an asshole. Dad and I drove Hayden to the hospital first, but when we got back we swept up all the pieces.

It wasn't long after that until it was my birthday, and to celebrate Dad took me out driving with him. It was the weekend, so we had plenty of time. Mom was home with Lorris playing Legos, because in a recent school art project his portrait of the family had her smaller than the rest of us, off in the corner. She'd been at work a lot. I don't think Lorris meant anything about it. He was always a terrible artist. But you could tell she was upset.

When we weren't rushed, Dad liked to pull out all the stops in the driving. First he drove us to the parking lot in Marine Park, and let me drive around there for a few minutes. We pulled into and out of vertical spaces. Everybody learned how to drive in the Marine Park parking lot, and the cops didn't mind as long as you were being safe. I've heard they're much more careful now—they jumped all over the two underage kids last week who ran their mother's car into a hydrant—but this was a while ago. We were particularly safe, of course, because we were in Dad's driving instructor car. It had a problem with the wheel so that it lilted a little to the left if you didn't correct it, but it was perfect and I loved it.

From there we pulled onto Quentin, rode that all the way down to Flatbush, which was heavy six-lane traffic. Dad took the wheel again at that point. I was still getting used to cars on both sides of me. He exaggerated all his driving motions here, the point being for me to observe. Hit the left blinker. Make sure you're keeping up with traffic. Always check all three mirrors.

If you stay on Flatbush and keep going you hit the water, Rockaway and the Atlantic, twenty blocks from our house, but that's getting onto the highway, and I didn't want to deal with that yet. We made a right onto U, and Dad stayed in the right lane the whole way. Then, after passing the public library and the salt marsh where the water mill used to be, where you can still see the foundation coming out of the surface, we were in Gerritsen. Dad ceremonially pulled into an open spot and put the car in park and pulled the keys out and handed them to me when we passed each other going around the hood.

This was my favorite moment, using the key, the throat-grumbling the engine makes when it comes on, how if you do it wrong it kick-starts like someone laughing hysterically. Then the way the wheel shakes a little in your hand, your foot on the brake, everything ready to move.

I pulled out and Dad said, Good, good, keep it easy, and I

imagined the fake line in the middle of the road like he told me to, keeping a little to the left of it. I hit my right blinker and we were on a one-way street, and my turn came perfectly into the center. I accelerated a little and tried to ease off and onto the break at the red light, completely smooth. I navigated around a double-parked car without my dad saying a word.

When we were little, the only activity that Lorris and I wanted every night was wrestling with Dad. He didn't like to hit us; Mom was the one we were afraid of, her slaps more damaging than any neighborhood scrape. Scarier too because she'd cry after, holding ice to our cheeks, even though we told her it was OK and we didn't need the ice. But wrestling was something that Dad knew how to do. He'd lie down in our living room on his back, and one or the other of us would run down the hallway and take a running leap and jump on top of him. Then the other would come from behind his head and try to cover his eyes or hold his legs. When we jumped, he made an *oof* sound, like we had knocked the air out, but he always caught us, in midair, no matter what part of him we tried to jump on top of. He'd keep us suspended there for a few seconds, turning us back and forth like a steering wheel, and then pull us back down and wrap our arms in a pretzel. Mom liked to watch this from the kitchen, where she'd be cleaning the dishes, usually Dad's job but she let him off the hook when he was wrestling with us.

Coming down a one-way street like that was the same feeling of being suspended in midair, the windows open, the radio off so I could concentrate, the car on a track, almost, so it felt impossible to deviate. I could close my eyes or shut off the driving part of my brain and the car would keep going forward, where I was willing it to go.

It was the corner, the one with two traffic lights, the one with the old storage warehouse on one side, and the Burger King, where teenagers go after the movies to sky the drink machines and not pay; with the shit factory on the other side, the green fence shaped like a wave on the top that goes on and on forever. There's a gate in the fence with an entrance to the recycling dump. When Dad saw it, it was like he woke up from being asleep with his eyes open. He leaned forward and said, Make a right here, go into there. We've got to pick something up. Then the red Chevy came screaming up from behind us and crunched into the passenger side.

I sat in the driver's seat. There were doors being opened and slammed shut. I think I heard the sirens immediately. Police cars were never far away. The Chevy driver went right over to Dad's side and pulled him out and Dad lay on the ground, breathing heavy, on his back, looking up.

I was in the car. I was out of the car. I was sitting on the side of the curb. My dad lay on his back and groaned quietly, talking to himself. There were people all around him. He kept pushing the air in front of him, up and away. My mom got there. My dad was sitting up. She was screaming the whole time. Another fucking air conditioner, she said. Driving with your fucking underage son. You've got some fucking lot of nerve. Dad was sitting up and laughing. He was shaking his head, I remember that. He'd just gotten a haircut, and you could see red skin beneath the gray. I remember when Dad came to say good night to us, later, he said, Your mother and I love each other very much. He had his hands on the side of the mattress. Don't take things so seriously, he said.

It was hot that night, and Lorris was in my room again. Mom pulled out the trundle bed. She smoothed the sheets. She kept her hand on his cheek, her other hand on my arm, her feet between the two beds, until Lorris told her that he wanted to turn on the other side. She went downstairs, and she put the television on, but we could hear her and Dad arguing. They were quiet. We only heard the sounds of their voices. It stopped soon and they turned the television off. Lorris got out of the pullout bed and stood in front of mine. He put his hand on the side, and I lifted up the sheet. I faced one way, and he faced the other, because I didn't like it when our breaths hit, but he kept his foot next to mine until four in the morning. Then he got up to go to the bathroom, and I had the bed and the sheets and the quiet room to myself.

OPEN YOUR EYES

Sitting on the bus on the way home from Kings Highway train station with our shopping bags at our feet, Lorris pointed at the man sitting across from us. It was the years when we fought. Look, Lorris said. When the man reached down to scratch his lower leg his jeans rode up a little, and you could see his gun, just the holster and the leather strap. He's a policeman, I told Lorris. Lorris nodded. I feel safe, he said.

We fought all the time. We threw punches. We kneed each other in the chest. We knocked each other down, waited until the other one got up, knocked him down again. We got angry. We squeezed each other's fingers so hard they got jammed, or what looked like jammed, in the way that we jammed our fingers while playing basketball. We scratched pimples into our legs and called them mosquito bites.

When fights were over, when Lorris was knocked down, when I had my whole weight on top of him, I gave what was our cruelest punishment of all—the kiss of death—the bone of my chin jammed into his cheek, pushed down between his gums until he screamed, hard enough that they'd stay raw, and the orthodontist, when Lorris went to one a few years later, told Lorris he needed braces.

But when I pulled my chin away, he gave me the same look, his eyes disdainful, as if he knew there was nothing else I could do. And, surprised, I'd let him up.

Then we'd lean against the wall together, breathing hard. It stopped us being angry. We could be regular human beings then, so much that by the time our father came running up the stairs, shouting, What's going on? we'd be laughing, or doing something else, my glasses crooked but back on my face.

Every year we went shopping at Christmastime, by ourselves, near Kings Highway. There were stores for everything. Rainbow for clothing, KB Toys, a small bookstore, jewelry shops. Once I went by myself but came back ten minutes later than I'd said I would, and my mother had been sitting next to the door, on a dining room chair. My father was pacing the room. Lorris was watching out the window, and it was him who opened the door.

You're fucked, he said, quietly, happily, the emphasis too much on the second word. With his body blocking my parents' view, he punched me above the knee, and backed quickly away, so I had to hobble into the house. From then on Lorris and I went together, even though it wasn't clear what good Lorris would do. Two's better than one, our father said, and left it at that.

One winter, not long after that—on our first stop we got clothes. A turtleneck for our mother, who was trying to start running even with the snow, and a sweatshirt for our father, because he said he looked good in them. Then we went to the bookstore under the train tracks.

Morning, we said, as we entered the shop. The bell had rung over our heads. The man grunted. Good morning, Lorris said, stamping on the welcome mat in front of the door, with pictures of snowflakes on its edges. The man looked up but didn't grunt. We spread out around the store, opening books and looking at their inside covers. Here, Lorris said, and handed me a small red one: *Walking Tours of Brooklyn*. Perfect, I said. One more. Mister, I said, do you have any suggestions for a gift for our father.

The owner of the bookstore looked at us. He was reading the paper. The headline rustled into the subheadline while the owner shuffled. Is he still married? the owner asked. I said yes. The shop owner kept reading his paper.

In between two rows of books, Lorris put a hand on my shoulder and pointed at the ground. Look, he said. I looked down. Then he reached up and slapped my ear, and it started ringing. He danced away before I could grab him, but I threw the book I was holding at his neck. He shifted and it hit his shoulder, and the pages flapped to the ground. Hey, the shop owner said, but Lorris was already laughing. He dodged out of the store, and the bell clanged over his head. I found a book of best travel destinations with a pretty woman on the cover and bought that. Lorris was standing outside, and I pushed him against a car. The sound of his body hitting the front made a satisfying thud, and then we were better. The week-old snow had left streaks of dirt and frost on the car's window, and Lorris's body left a print.

I wanted to get Lorris a pair of sneakers with wheels in them that you could pop out, instant rollerblades. So we went into Payless, me leading and pulling Lorris behind, his eyes closed. When I asked the salesman where to look, I did so in a whisper, so that Lorris couldn't hear. Once I'd paid, I led him outside, and stood him there, and just looked at him for a second. He was small against the Payless window, his head only coming up a little above the display shelf of shoes. Breathing in and out, he had his hands flattened, calmly, against his side. People walking by were starting to look at us. Ready, I said.

Then Lorris said, Now it's my turn. While I closed my eyes he turned me around, around, and around again, his head coming up only to my chin. The sounds of the world came at me, the gray snow on the sidewalk receding into nothing.

Eyes closed, I could hear my breath more rapidly. It came on alternate beats with my footsteps, the crunch on the salted cement. Lorris's hand, never touching me, pulled at my jacket sleeve, and I stumbled forward. I could hear people shouting, though I wasn't sure why. A truck beeped near us, and there was the slide that comes when a car pulls into a spot, just missing the curb. The tires hugged the ground. Lorris, I said. He didn't answer. I smelled the tang of lemon, from the falafel restaurant, the burning of the legs of meat I remembered must be turning, slowly, in the window.

What happened then, I can only describe it as a vision. It appeared in my eyelids like a movie, with surround sound, circling my head. In the vision, Lorris and I were in a car, and he was driving. He didn't feel older, he was just driving, as if he knew how and it was natural. It was an old car, the dashboard dusty and streaked with fingerprints. I was in the passenger seat, leaning back. Maybe I was teaching him—though I didn't know how, though it felt like I did. Lorris made turn after turn. I didn't recognize where we were, but it was a one-way street. Ahead of us, there was a speed bump, and on top of the speed bump, something small wrapped in blankets. We got closer, and I saw the blankets shift. There was the sound of the tires on the unevenly paved street, the hum. The echo of the blinker click as it shut off. Lorris was looking straight ahead. When we went over the speed bump, there was another sound. Was that—, Lorris said. No, I lied. I told him no. You're fine. It was nothing. Lorris looked at me, pleading. The car stopped at the end of the street. He put it into park. He put his hands back on the wheel. Other cars passed us, slowed down, sped up, there were those sounds—but he wouldn't look away. Then the vision ended, and the real Lorris was saying, in the real world, Open your eyes.

We waited for the bus for fifteen minutes. Lorris had his bags arranged on the sidewalk around him. He showed me his palms, where the stretched plastic had cut into them, leaving a deep red trench. He held them up to me and I wouldn't answer him at first. Rub them, I said.

A pregnant woman smiled at us from two people ahead in the line. I looked down at the ground. Happy holidays, she said. I nodded. How old is he? she asked. Old enough, I said. Lorris was kneeling down, checking with one hand in each bag that everything from his packages was still there. How long is your bus ride? she asked. Five and a half minutes, Lorris said, his eyes still on his bags on the ground.

It felt wrong going up the bus steps, watching Lorris, ahead of me, using his MetroCard next to the driver. The bus felt too heavy, Lorris too close to the wheel. I closed my eyes and tried to listen. The bus engine coughed. People muttered in the front seats. I opened my eyes, and reached up toward Lorris one step above me. Let's walk, I said. Or take the next one. Please. Lorris looked down the steps. He gave me the scathing look again, like he did when I hit him, like there was no way he could hurt. Then he turned and got on the bus. I watched him go. You coming? the bus driver asked.

The avenues began to pass by. We sat next to each other, not talking. I leaned back. The bus engine coughed and coughed. The man with the jeans reached down to scratch his leg, showed the gun. Safe, Lorris said.

———

This all happened and we got to the house and in half an hour both our parents would be home, having left to walk to the mall on the other side of Avenue R to buy presents for us, not holding hands but with their hands almost touching, swinging side by side. But there was no way for us to know that then, standing at the front door leaning on the bell. We could hear the sound of it echoing. The windows were all closed. The echo came back to us, like laughing. A tall man on a too-small bike came riding slowly down the sidewalk. He was careening side to side. He looked at us, kept watching us until he was all the way on the other end of the block, and then he stopped, and looked back. Let's go, Lorris, I said.

Walking quickly, we went around through the alley to the back of the house, opened the red gate. I reached around in the plastic case over the barbecue, found the key I hid there, went to open the back door. The locks clicked. Hello? I asked the house. The basement was damp and smelled like summer. Nothing answered. I locked the door behind us.

I turned to Lorris and put one finger to my lips, and we walked up the creaking stairs. The house was quiet. One open window, off the kitchen, let some air in, and the curtain fluttered. I turned on the light, which hissed. Hello? I said again.

The bottom of the curtain was dancing. It was a dark curtain, I don't know why we had dark curtains. It seemed heavier than it should be. I couldn't see behind it. The curtain kept dancing. Slowly we walked toward it. I could hear everything from outside, the scrape of a door, the sound of people running, a horn beeping, twice. I raised my hands, I felt my knuckles pop. And suddenly there was a hand grabbing my arm and I turned around and swung.

It was Lorris, laughing, who ducked the punch, and ran shrieking into the living room, but I followed him, running, threw him down on the floor and hit him with both hands. His stomach, so the wind got knocked out, his shoulders, his face with my palms. He was shouting, scratching at me, my face, my mouth, my eyes. The packages were strewn around us. I pinned him, so he couldn't move anything, and leaned my head down close to his. Close your eyes, I said. No, he said, get off me. But then I hit him again and he did. I did too. I could hear the creaking of the walls, the rush of the bus going by outside the windows. There were no leaves for the wind to rustle on the dead trees. Lorris whispered, What are you going to do?

VINCENT AND AURORA

They had lived alone together for many years, since their sons moved out to get married. It was a house on Madoc Avenue, where the backyard opened onto the water, and a wooden dock extended from the porch out into Dead Horse Bay. In the summers they left their motorboat there, the *Napoli*, and they'd take it up and down the canal, past the salt marsh, its high grass and swampy inlets, sometimes all the way out to Rockaway, under the Marine Parkway Bridge.

They weren't rich and they weren't poor, although when Vincent turned sixty-five their children, Tommy and Salvy, threw him a surprise party and sent a check for five hundred dollars. Aurora wanted to rip it up. Vincent collected Social Security and she had always saved her earnings, from working at the voting polls at PS 222 for decades. Democrat or Republican? she'd ask, and hand them a white sheet or blue sheet. This year it was Bush and Clinton. Vincent had had his candy store, but then he'd sold it to the Benduccis. At Christmas, they always had a live tree.

The house was painted white, with little flecks where tree branches had kicked off color during storms, and a flat roof that the kids liked to go onto when they were teenagers. Once Vincent found cans of PBR in the gutter when he was cleaning out the leaves, and he sat his sons down to talk to them more about their indiscretion than anything else. It surprised them, his sudden sharpness, all the more so when they found that he wasn't angry about the beer. Who hadn't tried to get away from their parents on a summer night, the breeze coming off the water, the sky clear to Manhattan, Vincent had put it. He understood. But where he was raised, in Carroll Gardens, with the Irish cops, you had to be more careful—and he wanted them to understand this, to take a certain amount of care. He didn't tell Aurora about the beer.

It was a row house, connected to other houses on the side, differentiated from a suburb, though you'd be hard-pressed for what to call it. Marine Park was the part of the city, Aurora often said, least served by the train and bus system. If the oceans rose like people said they would, this part of Brooklyn would be the first to go. It was an hour with the walk to the Q train and the ride into the city to see a Broadway play, or to go to the Museum of Natural History, which meant lower real estate prices and a bit of sleepiness. One neighbor was a drug addict, supported by unknown funds. There was the neighborhood drunk, who was in and out of the house. Across the street the eldest son of a large family—who marked his adolescent growth year after year with new tattoos, sprouting in strange places across his body, reported one after another by a gleeful Tommy, who knew him from school—was gone one day after the Fourth of July: two years in jail. Their true neighbor, just to the left, shoveled snow for them if they woke up too late in the morning. He lived alone, and needed neither conversation nor pleasantries. He'd taken in their mail when they went to Canada for a week, years before. They stayed in Montreal, and then a few days in a cabin next to Lake Oromocto, where Vincent had gone fishing in the mornings and Aurora spent a small amount of time depressed on the back porch, then getting better in the afternoons, making penne vodka and a salad. When the children were born they did not travel.

When they were younger Vincent spent most of the day at the candy shop. Aurora stayed home. Besides the poll work, she mended clothes and tailored suits. For Halloween season she made the kids' costumes from scratch. Salvy especially had liked to watch her sew, and for a while she got him interested in it, sewing his own moccasins like the Lenni Lenape Indians—who had lived right where their house was, she told him, those very blocks. They'd had a permanent settlement, and sometimes people found bits of wampum under the dirty sand by the water, and Salvy liked to dig for them and bring them back to Aurora, who had an open fascination with history and geology and the way things got buried and preserved.

Tommy was more Vincent's son, even though when he grew up he became a banker, and after school he would go straight to the candy store on Ocean and Twenty-Sixth. Tommy would scratch the top of his head against his father's lips and then hide in the comic book section. He liked to stand by the turning pedestal of greeting cards and write obscene things inside them when Vincent wasn't looking, and once this got Vincent into trouble, when a customer came back with an anniversary card in his hand and loosened his jacket to show the .22 on his belt, sticking his tongue into the corner of his lip. That was after Korea, after returning soldiers had gone to the Fire Academy or cop school and moved in droves to their neighborhood in Gerritsen Beach, and sometimes they forgot they weren't in Pusan even though it was years ago.

Tommy and Salvy still came to visit a few times a month. Tommy came every Sunday. The boys came in their sports cars with Italian bread and cookies from a bakery on Smith Street, where Aurora used to go for lemon ices. Salvy had married a Russian girl, but Vincent and Aurora didn't care, as long as the wives helped out with the dishes between courses. In the kitchen Aurora labored over sauce. Vincent had once been a heavy drinker, but now he was happy with two glasses of pinot grigio at dinner. The wine enlivened his senses a little, then dulled them. He didn't think there was anything wrong with this. From where he sat at the head of the table he could see Aurora, her hands folded in her lap if she wasn't taking bites. She cleared the table; he did the dishes. The boys and their wives left. She sat in the living room and had the TV on, though she wasn't really watching, more like meditating. The sound of the faucet drowned out the rest of the day. In the kitchen, it was Vincent's daily ritual, his back turned to the rest of the house and his attention focused on the white wall in front of him, the metal sink. He washed dishes slowly, one after the other. If he let the wine glass sit without washing it, the dry dregs grew crusted, stuck on the side of the cup.

One evening, not long after Vincent's sixty-fifth birthday, he got a phone call, the first of its kind in a while, late at night when Aurora was upstairs reading a biography and he was half-asleep in front of the television. It was large and monstrous, sticking out hideously into the center of the room, but the boys had bought it for them, Father's Day that year. Vincent wasn't used to how real it sounded, what a presence it was. He had thought the phone call was coming from the TV.

He walked over to the kitchen where the family phone was attached to the wall, flicked the kitchen light on, and picked up the receiver. When he did, he heard in the background the oddly amplified sound of waves lapping. Along with the static of the connection, it was strangely familiar, reminiscent of something that made Vincent's fingers start tapping on the counter.

Use the other phone, Vin, the voice said. Three minutes.

Vincent hung the phone back up on the wall and sat down slowly on one of the kitchen stools. He looked at the scratches made on the table from the bottom of the coffeemaker that they used every morning. He traced the scratches with his nails. Then he walked over to the refrigerator and poured himself orange juice.

When he finished every drop in the glass, the light coating of pulp still on the upper half, he went back into the living room and sat in his recliner, his corner of the room where Aurora never cleaned. He turned the volume on the television up. Then he reached under the seat cushion and pulled out a mobile.

Before the news went to commercial the mobile began to beep, and he pressed a button with his thumb and held the phone up to his ear.

What if Rory had picked up? he said quietly.

It's been a long time, Vin, said Benducci.

Call like that again without letting me know and I'll give you a what-for.

It's been a long time, Benducci said again.

You're telling me.

What was it, the *Maria*?

Not the *Calabrese*? I thought that was the summer before.

Good to hear your voice, Vin.

Upstairs Vincent heard the radio turn off, and he banged his elbow on the chair arm rushing to hide the phone, but brought it back up to his ear when the bedroom door didn't open.

OK? asked Benducci.

I could be talking to anyone, Vincent said. I don't talk to anyone much from before anymore.

Benducci let that rest and then said, Nice and quiet.

Not too bad.

You could use a little excitement.

Vincent laughed from his lungs and wiped the corner of his mouth. Not really, he said.

You could use a little extra money with the roof needing a fix. Vincent kept laughing. It never surprised him what type of research the capos in charge of guys like Benducci did. Or had access to, he supposed. It was the way they had liked to work. The roof *had* been leaking enough that even Vincent cleaning out the gutter hadn't helped. Benducci laughed too.

Listen, Bendy, what do you need? I think the roof'll be just fine, but if it's not a big job maybe I can help you out.

It's another boat job.

Like I know anything else? Why me?

Nobody does these anymore. The money's from Wall Street now. Nobody knows Brooklyn.

What's the bag?

Silver dollars.

As in from the infomercials?

They're twenty per.

Sounds fair.

And we bring it down to Red Hook.

While they went over the details Vincent's mind wandered. He was excited. Not excited, but a something-to-wake-up-for-in-the-morning feeling. He'd been running numbers with his little brothers since his uncle was the numbers man for South Brooklyn. Put money down on the last digit of the winnings that day at the racetrack, and adolescent Vincent would come to your house and give you your purse, or just a shake of the head. It was a living then, a way to make something on the side, and he'd always liked spending it in the candy store, chocolate or soda here and there. Eventually he started driving, and Idlewild Airport had just been finished, before it was JFK, and you could make real money driving cars and trucks parked on those lonely watery roads, heavy with cargo that disappeared from the belly of planes, down the LIE and the BQE to the warehouse sections of the borough, as long as you weren't curious enough to ask any questions. He made enough to buy the candy store. He made enough to buy the *Napoli*, and when the truck jobs became too common he was right in place to put the boat to service, hauling boxes of watches, designer jewelry, sometimes plain money, from the empty junkyards right where the runways hit the water. He never knew too much. Sometimes they didn't land, just pulled up alongside unmarked, unnamed boats, Coast Guard cruisers conspicuously absent. Once he saw a man get shot in the leg, and it was the smell of it that unnerved him. Once when he made a wise comment someone hit him in the face, and when he acted surprised, he remembered the strange look Benducci gave him, as if there was something about Vincent he couldn't understand. The black eye turned blue, then green. But he knew how to put those things out of his head. He had done fine, better than his father, who trimmed off the garbage scows leaving the Navy Yard for a dollar a day.

In the morning he'd get all his things together, the painters' gloves, the fake papers. It was just going out on the boat, and he wasn't that old that he couldn't handle the water. Everyone always said he looked fifteen years younger. Tommy and Salvy wouldn't be around for another week. Otherwise he'd be going for a long walk by the water in the morning and lying on the couch until Aurora finished making dinner. She wouldn't say a word to him until they sat at the table, when she would pleat her hands together and gesture at the plates. Now, she would say, and begin to serve. Retirement and an empty house were fine, but it was nice to do something once in a while. He sat at the kitchen counter, poured himself a finger from a bottle of white wine. He swirled, he drank.

————————

Aurora was upstairs when the signal went off, silently, next to her bed lamp. It was a light plugged into the back of her wake-up clock, hidden from Vincent's side, that blinked yellow when it needed to. At first she forgot what it was, felt like she was in a dream: something you remember from a long time ago, a cousin you haven't seen in years. Watch him fall off a motorcycle in a dreamscape and break his hand, everything else miraculously fine, wake up in the morning and pick up the phone to call and ask if he's OK. Stop, she said to herself now. It can't be real.

Aurora shifted her weight from one side of the mattress to the other and looked at the light, which had already stopped blinking yellow. What was the failure rate of these lightbulbs? she thought to herself. What if it's just mechanically faulty? But she could hear the volume going up on the nightly news, the Channel 5 story of Manny the truck driver, who won the lottery this weekend by a stroke of luck. This should be around the time when Vin was falling asleep, this hour, close to it, and there was no other reason for the television to be on so loud, and her light going off, unless.

She'd been dropping a suit off in the Garment District when they approached her. In Colin's Bar and Grill they showed her the badge under the table. Told her that this was an opportunity, historic, to do something important. And Vincent didn't need to know because they weren't interested in Vincent. They knew he was a decent guy. She just had to tell them when the shipments came in, and where they were going. The airport was a leaky faucet, and for a while it had been open season from the storage facilities. When she said she'd have to think about it, the detective with the pimple under his mustache said, Think quick, because we take him in if you don't. She said, I've never heard anything about any of this. The detective scratched his pimple and waited.

At first she was angry, and she refused to cook. She told Vincent she was sick. Then she bottled it in. Everything's fine. They were young when they got married, he a few years out of high school. What did they know? She'd had one steady, Anthony Thomas, whom she'd kissed once in an alleyway. Vincent was nicer than him, spoke softer and took her to restaurants, brought her things from his uncle's candy store.

He was good but the two of them were different, like the Canada trip had shown. A half century of marriage, and they'd traveled out of the country once. He spent the whole time on a motorboat they had rented, going from one side of the lake to the other, ferrying back and forth. He'd come back, be happy, having been outside all day, feeling refreshed. She didn't call the phone number like she usually did for that one. She had thought they might get away from it. She had thought they were on vacation.

Why did she do it? How does it feel to make dinner every day and three courses on Sunday? How many times did she actually work the polls? Five, six times a year? And she'd always loved the gangster stories—Diamond Jim out in Chicago, who owned all the brothels, and how the government took him down. It's the type of thing that you keep doing, out there in the white house by the water and the highway. Sometimes she hated that house. Nothing going on. So much he didn't know. The amount of money you make for poll work. He'd never voted in his life.

She got up in the morning and cleaned up the bedroom, came downstairs around ten. Vincent was already sitting at the kitchen counter with his coffee. She scrubbed each dish twice, her back to his.

Nice day, he said. Thinking about going to get the oil changed on the Toyota.

Aurora patted him on the back of his neck, got the orange juice out of the refrigerator.

Nice day for a drive, he said. Or a boat ride. Haven't taken her out in a bit.

Sure, she said, and then she knew.

Just really one of those days, no? Nice morning days?

Like out on the lake in Canada.

Sort of, he said. But it's nicer here. Everything is clearer.

True. She poured him some more juice.

When Vincent got to the candy store at two the next afternoon, the CLOSED sign was already swinging on the door to the shop. He went in and there was Benducci, sitting behind the cash register.

You lost a little hair, Vincent said.

It's the insurance payments, said Benducci as he came around the counter to say hello. They embraced, Vincent's palm on Benducci's back. He could feel the skin over his bones.

They used to do them together, the jobs. Benducci was younger, and they always sent him with Vincent because Benducci was the muscle, on the off chance that something went wrong. Benducci had this Italian surname, but his family had been in America for generations, uncles of his always telling stories about the way it was before the guineas got here. They were a southern family. Benducci had a southern belle sister that everyone in the neighborhood knew: her name was Everleigh, a family tradition. An aunt far back on a plantation used to sign her letters, Everly Yours.

They sat on the stools. Vincent spread his arms and laughed.

Look at me, he said. I'm too old for this garbage. He pointed at Benducci. You too.

Come on, sixty-five is basically sixty, and then you're in your fifties, he said. And that's just middle-aged.

That's the optimist talking.

Honestly, I haven't done a job in years, and I got excited. He opened his hands. Who else would I call?

Vincent walked around to the Coke machine and took a can. Benducci eyed him. You gonna pay for that?

Vincent put a quarter on the counter.

They're a little more now.

So. Under the Parkway Bridge, seven thirty?

Just offshore, right where people fish.

They'll be no one on the bridge?

I'm heading over right now to put up some signs and talk to people.

Anyway, no one ever notices.

Benducci didn't answer.

Anything I should know?

Should be fine. The boat's a twenty-footer, they'll have two handlers too. No cops. Any cruisers, we split. Supposed to be important that the drop point doesn't get found, it's the last warehouse in Red Hook that the cops don't know about. But if it stays clear tonight it won't be a problem, we can see all the way to Breezy Point.

Vincent rubbed his knee and drank his Coke and kept his head nodding while Benducci was talking.

She followed him out to the candy store. She took the Chevy, gray and easy to miss. Parked it two blocks up on the opposite side of the street, watched the entrance from her side-view mirror. Then she drove to Good Shepherd church to go to confession.

When was your last confession, my child?

Jimmy? It's me.

Rory?

The booth was dark, and there was a piece of pink gum stuck on the underside of the seat. It was always Monsignor Jim at this hour of the day, and he'd been doing it for years, since back when the pews were full every Sunday. Jim's brother was a police lieutenant, and he'd been working with Aurora since the beginning.

How do you know it's a boat job?

He was talking with Benducci, that's all they'd ever do. They always leave after dinner.

Aren't you guys a little old for this?

Isn't that what you tell the kids when they punch their brothers?

No, I tell them to read the smutty magazines.

That's not even funny, Monsignor.

They were quiet for a moment, and the church was quiet the way it is on Tuesday afternoons. Aurora could hear people walking by outside the stained-glass windows.

I'll tell my brother, he said. Don't worry, they'll stay far back and just figure out where they're going. His side of the box was silent for a moment. Strange, he said.

Aurora looked at her watch. There had been one time when she almost told Vin, after a job one cold December right after Salvy was born. They sat together on the porch when he got back (she had been in the kitchen; he came in from the "groceries," said he needed a little fresh air) and they watched the gray clouds on the water. It wasn't pretty that time of year, but it was powerful. The sky always so heavy. She had her hand around his arm and she almost confessed everything. They could have found a way to make it right. But the words were wrong, and the two of them so recently parents. So she made him a sandwich, and then Tommy was born, and they grew up, and Vincent went out on the boat less and less, until he didn't go out at all. And when it was all over, what was the point of telling stories?

Did I do the right thing coming? she said.

The Monsignor breathed into the screen.

Do you feel that you've done wrong?

Sometimes.

Do you regret lying to your husband?

Of course.

I can't imagine what it was like.

Aurora didn't answer.

When it's over, make Vin a cup of coffee. And then tell him five times that you love him.

The Monsignor opened the screen. She looked at his face, bulbous and sweaty, and she realized suddenly how old he'd become. It was easier to think of him only as a voice. She opened the door. That's ridiculous, she said as she left.

It was one of those evenings after a hot summer day, where you could be sitting in the living room, the windows open, and all of a sudden the sound of the rain on the concrete. Outside, the streetlights blinking with the force of the rain. What could you expect in the morning but the trains all stopped, flooding the tracks—the abovegrounds, this far out in the borough? Cars stuck in the middle of Kings Highway, or under the F train high-rises, the Gowanus seeping onto dry land.

Dinner, Vincent doing the dishes, excusing himself to Aurora watching television to say that he was taking the *Napoli* out for a quick fish. Him on the boat, kicking it away from the wood dock, his fishing pole on his right, which he moves to the back once he's out of sight of the house, when he picks up Benducci in a blue sweatshirt.

She is sitting in the kitchen sipping coffee. This rain, she thought. He'll get soaked.

She's wearing a leopard-print blouse and tight black slacks, because that's what she likes to wear around the house.

He's feeling the cold now in his bones, but Benducci tosses him another coat and gives him a thumbs-up, says be careful of the swells.

She's sitting in bed with a book. She can hear the gutter flooding on the roof, and the window is that color of purple with the sun going down and the clouds and thunder. She is beginning to feel worried about Vincent seeing the police cruiser.

He's out past Deep Creek now, Dead Horse Bay, where there had been a glue factory once and they say you can still find the scraped-out hooves of horses buried in the dirt. You can just see the lights of the few cars by the Belt Parkway and, up ahead, the bridge, then thin Rockaway and the Atlantic.

The storm has become tremendous. She puts on a windbreaker and bangs the door shut. She forgets her wallet. She runs back in to get it. She walks quickly down the street, starts dragging her legs because it's not quick enough, to the Chevy, to drive to the open water. She gets in, fumbles with her keys, her hand on the passenger headrest while she backs up. Floors forward. She is moving now, and no one is out, the rain's too heavy—she can hardly see even with the wipers. She's on Flatbush Avenue, hitting all the lights. She is flying past Floyd Bennett Field, where Charles Lindbergh landed when he got back to America. The batting cages, the football fields, here the bridge coming up in front.

He's unloading, Benducci is passing him cardboard boxes. One rips at the top as they transfer, and he sees stacked packages of white powder. Bendy, he says, what the fuck is this? Benducci is looking out into the bay for boats. He looks at Vincent like he's crazy. It's for the clients, not money, he says. He takes a packet, slips it in his back pocket. On top of their bonuses. Vincent is staring at the boxes. He claws at the rip, looks at the piece of paper above the packages. WATER STREET, NEW YORK, NY, it says. And Vincent knows that he has broken his cardinal rule. *Don't look, don't care.*

Aurora parks next to the E-ZPass and starts running up the bike path, up the bridge, pulling her hood over her head. She's cold and she has that sick feeling in her chest that means she shouldn't be doing this right now, her lungs pumping, her feet on the pavement. She's not sure why she's here. She wants to tell him to leave it all alone. She's at the top and she sees the *Napoli* all the way below, pulling up next to a bigger boat, and she sees Vincent. And the police cruiser, too close, trying to stay within eyesight. She has the irrational idea that Vincent will know it's her if they see the cruiser. She almost feels his eyes staring through her. Vin! she yells. But he can't hear her. The rain is getting in her mouth.

She sees the cop boat coming around the bend, and then she comes down back off the bridge. On the shore she's waving her hands, her hat, and she can tell that Vin sees somebody, sees her; feels like she can feel his breath collapse as he heads to shore. She's waving and the cop cruiser is getting closer so you can see the blue markings on the side and they must have seen it by now and the *Napoli* pulls onto the sand and she runs to the bow.

Vin—, she says, but he cuts her off.

The hell are you doing here? he yells. He reaches out a hand to help her get in. He's no longer breathing right. Benducci pulls out a mobile and presses a button, yells into the phone, New location. Vinny's. Blues. Then he hangs up. She doesn't have time to remember that trip in Canada when Vincent used to pick her up by the crook of her knees and the meat of her back and throw her in the canoe they rented, before they pull away. Benducci is in the back, and under his arm he has a handgun. He pulls his hood over his head, and Aurora shivers down next to Vincent. The cop cruiser is getting closer, an NYPD SWAT team in black and blue. One of them is extending a finger and pointing at the *Napoli*.

At first Benducci doesn't mean it. He's holding the gun out in the rain and inspecting it when it discharges, and then he looks out to the cruiser. There are warning shots from them, and then Benducci is heaving side to side, gasping every time he pulls the trigger. He's shooting more than the cops, who look like they're just trying to get closer, but this is the *Napoli*, and she's a fine motorboat. Vincent hears the wind of a bullet as it passes by over their stern. They spit over open water to hug the islet next to the bay, and it's too close for the cops, who veer offshore. At some point Benducci has stopped heaving. Vincent makes a cut around the land barrier and the cruiser looks motionless, uncertain, so far behind.

At the dock, behind their white house, Aurora climbs up onto the wood. But Vincent is looking at Benducci, with his hands over the side next to the motor, one eye open and no longer breathing, his bloody mouth on the mounting bracket. Hell, he says. Shit, shit. He's crouching in the middle of the boat, and he slams a fist on the plastic siding. Bendy, goddamn. Aurora stands on the dock, her hands on opposite shoulders. The blood is all down Benducci's neck, and it has soaked his sweatshirt, though it's hard to tell from the rain. In death already his face has set, and there is an ugly, wet smell.

They turn when the motion-sensor light goes on. Out of the alleyway comes Tommy, who's holding a mobile in his hand. But then he stops.

Mom? he says.

And then they see the searchlights from the police cruiser

getting closer, a quarter mile away, and Tommy says, Get inside, and then he runs to the *Napoli* and jams the powerhead back. The blood that dripped from Benducci's neck is washed away by the wake of the *Napoli* leaving, and Vincent can see Benducci's gruesome dead hand, hanging over the side of the white boat where he had left it, in his last moments.

As the *Napoli* pulls away and the drone dies down, Vincent and Aurora watch in the rain, before they go into the house. Vincent keeps opening and closing his fists, to feel them still numb. They watch from the back porch as the *Napoli* flees into the salt marsh, where the Lenni Lenape hunting grounds used to be, where their bones were buried and the boys used to catch tadpoles off the back of the boat, on family excursions. They can tell from the way the searchlights are flitting around and around that the cruiser is stationary, looking for the *Napoli* in the tall reeds and the stormy dark. But they do not know the salt marsh, and they do not enter its depths. Then the cruiser turns around and heads for Rockaway, Beach Channel, where everyone knows the Mob holes up today, at the edge of civilization. And Tommy, perhaps Tommy knows this.

They go inside. It is an old house. The tree branches are scratching against the siding. In the dark it looks run-down. It won't be until almost morning, when the storm is spread over only half the sky, the city clearing up, that Tommy will nudge the boat back into its home slip—once the police are gone, the body disappeared and sunk in the swamp, the boat clean and empty—the motor off for the last hundred meters, like he used to cut it when he was a teenager and his parents slept. Vincent can't imagine that time. He knows it will be upon him. It's a funny thing, the succession of things happening. He knows that he can sit in his chair and do nothing, and still in the morning Tommy will come home, and explain himself, or else the police will come with strange, sad looks in their eyes. He knows that he has the power to wait for it, and that waiting alone is his one hopeful thing.

They have lived in this house for a long time. There is the water through the window, the rain on the deck. Inside, the table counters are dry, and the house is warm and empty. It is the type of empty that has a sound, like white noise, a soft light over the armchair. When Aurora puts two fingers on Vincent's hand, nothing changes; the world outside rains and sleeps. Aurora leaves her fingers tentatively on Vincent's hand, so long that sweat begins to grow between their skins. Her arm begins to feel heavy, to cramp up, and the skin hangs down as if she is old, truly old. She has a vision of it, of no longer retaining control over her body, of her mind, slowly, being the last thing, dimming in, dimming out. Finally her finger feels like one part of Vincent's hand, and her arm is numb, and she wouldn't dream of moving it. Vincent stares straight forward, and it is the only communication she knows she can expect from him.

But in his head he's remembering when Tommy was a boy and he put antibiotic cream on his cut knee. How Tommy said it burned, and how he told Tommy, Stop crying. She thinks about how there was a very specific type of candy that Vin used to stock in the store, twenty years ago, but she can't remember the name now: just the chocolate taste, the peanut tang, a blue wrapper on the floor. How they took a box of them to the lake in Canada, eating them, one by one, while the miles marched by. In that moment, in the car, she remembers thinking about dancing. Outside, it gets wetter and wetter. It is an old house. The roof sometimes leaks. The walls creak with human sounds. The children's bedrooms are made up like they're about to come home.

WHY DON'T YOU

My father was born at the bottom of a hill: in a basement, where the landlord didn't allow visitors. He had brown fingers, even then. At the top of the hill was where the mafia lived, or at least the rich people. It went down in wealth from there. He liked to say this at dinner. Feel more sorry for yourself, why don't you, my mother said. She threw salad on his plate. Lorris had his fork and knife in his hand. I left, or I would leave, or I walked out again.

Natalia and I drank Coca-Cola in the oval in Marine Park. People played cricket there, between the baseball fields, but later it emptied out, and we brought drinks from the Russian teahouse. Inside they only used plastic cups, even though it was a nice restaurant. We mixed the soda with vodka from the liquor store down the block. On weekends, when she had no homework, we went into the city, to Times Square, no transfer on the Q. At the Marriott Marquis we rode the glass elevators up and down. We kissed pushed up against the glass, watching the hotel lounge get small below us. On every fifth floor there were platforms where you could see the lobby and Forty-Second Street. It's incredible, isn't it? Natalia said. It's like from an airplane. The cars were black and small from so far up. We stood with our noses pressed against the double windowpane and watched the lights change on Broadway. In Brooklyn, in the middle of the park, the cars on the avenues sounded like waves.

I met Natalia one night, at a friend's house, out in Sheepshead Bay. It was an exact replica of Marine Park, except the houses were smaller and closer together. We picked up forties from the corner store next to the House of Calamari, and my friend, who was born in Moscow, used a fake Russian passport to buy our beer. Why don't you get a fake ID like a normal person? I asked him. He muttered in Russian. When he went back to Moscow, the one time, he told me once, people had tried to kidnap him, but when he answered in their own language they started laughing and shouting. They offered him a sandwich and let him go. It was thick bread, one layer of spreading. We sat in his parents' basement and drank from coffee mugs, listening quietly to his mother yelling at his father upstairs. He turned his head up to the ceiling like he was baring his neck. Shut the fuck up! Company. There were other Russians there, and they didn't react, and all of them spoke English.

Natalia came with four other girls, and they all had dresses on. The only girls who wore dresses at our high school were from Russia. They all gave my friend and the other Russians kisses on the cheek, but they shook my hand, except for Natalia, who pulled me close so I could smell her hair. Hello, she said quietly. She was from Rockaway, but because the schools were so bad there, her parents drove her in to Madison. The only thing they knew about Madison was that U.S. senators were graduates. Three, but it didn't mean much of anything. They'd been musicians in Russia, but here they were computer engineers.

We were doing bar curls with the exercise equipment that my friend had in his basement. I was skinny from running track. The girls sat at the table with the plastic cover and played cards. We were outside, kneeling in his backyard, the smell of rain and fresh dirt around us, the smoke curling up to the second floor, the tendrils out of his open mouth. Here, he said. Come on. The toilet porcelain was cool and fresh when I laid my head against it, between heaves. Only Natalia knocked on the door, and whispered to ask if I needed something. For a moment I thought I did, but I didn't know what to tell her.

The walk home was cold, though I didn't feel it. When I woke up still clutching the toilet, and came out of the bathroom, my friend was asleep, lying with his back on the floor, the other Russians clustered around him. Two of the girls were on the couches, and one was in the middle of the Russians' embrace. Natalia was asleep with her head against the wall. I put my shoes on without waking anyone, and when I left the screen door banged, and I couldn't find the Q train. I worried that I hadn't locked the door, and that someone would break in and it would be my fault. I asked a strange figure for directions, and my voice sounded wrong in my ears. He didn't know. When I got home, the light was starting, and the old faces on the trees stared me down. Lorris woke me up, hanging on my shoulder, saying that I was supposed to hit him ground balls in the park. He woke up early, and did push-ups between meals. He wanted to make varsity when he got to high school. That morning I told him I was too tired, and he left without asking again, taking the bucket of balls to hit off the tee. I only asked for Natalia's number the next Monday at school, from my friend who hadn't asked how I got home. He pulled his phone out of his pocket along with the fake passport. It didn't look real, even though I'd never seen a Russian passport. Here, he said. But do you want it?

We would stretch out on the grass, so that just our heads were next to each other. We came here often. On the ground, looking up, you could pretend there was nothing but sky. She reached her hands behind her to cover my ears, and I did the same with hers, and reached farther down until they were on either side of her neck. She got up and we stood together, her hands clasped on my back, trying to push me through her. We didn't kiss. With my head on her shoulder I could see the water, the Marine Parkway Bridge in the heat-fog, where the ocean started and the city ends. Let's go to my house, she said. I couldn't talk, so I just squeezed her wrists.

Avenue U, the cars on all sides, where I was learning to drive without my father. The instructor, from another company, was a Vietnam vet who wanted to get into Republican politics. He let me into four-lane traffic even though I wasn't ready. I told her about it. We made it to Kimball without letting go of each other's sides. The B89 wasn't running for the weekend, so we took car service instead. In the backseat, she sat in the middle, me on the end, and she put her bag on my lap. Her hand went underneath. I held it there for a little, then let it go. The driver was listening to a station with words I didn't understand.

She was looking out the window. Motorboats went by on our left. Flatbush Avenue to the Parkway Bridge that goes to Rockaway and out toward the Hamptons. We didn't want to know anyone who lived in the Hamptons. Summers, I'd thought about going there, somewhere right on the tip: bike out or borrow someone's old Camry, sleep in the backseat; have one sleeping bag and throw it on top of us all unfolded, like a tent we hadn't battened down. We drove past the hangars, the empty Air Force land where nothing grew. The bridge hummed beneath us. Her parents' apartment, over Riis Park, before the houses started.

I paid the driver. We took the stairs up. Her keys in the door and the voices of her family, her parents and sister. They were in the kitchen, and I just walked straight to her room. When she came through the door she closed it, and turned the lock. On the edge of the sheets, she put a hand over my mouth. They're having dinner, she said. I hadn't taken my jeans off. We stand by the curtains and start all over again. We go slowly. The lifeguards are gone from the beach. Their chairs are bare and flecked with paint. Her hair smells like sand, like the worn sea glass Lorris collected when he was little, to put in jelly jars, the blunt edges never scratching the glass. *I see another*, he would shout, making constellations in his palm. *There's another*, with the glass grainy in his hands. *Another, there's another.*

VAMPIRE DEER ON
JEKYLL ISLAND

They were just getting out of dinner at the Jekyll Island Club Hotel Grand Dining Hall, the one where jackets are recommended, where the places of origin of the waiters are written on their golden name tags: Hungary, Kenya, Mozambique. Courtney had had too much to drink, gin and tonics, and Timothy was watching her as she navigated the steps, leaning on the wicker railing.

I'm fine, she said.

At the bottom of the stairs, Timothy waved off the valet, who was rummaging for the keys to their BMW. The valet stopped rummaging. The BMW had been one of the nicer cars in the lot, which surprised Timothy. Courtney was walking ahead of him, toward the water. He took long steps to catch up to her. When he did, she was stopped in the middle of the road, watching six deer stumble gracefully across.

Are those deer? Timothy asked, happily.

Of course they're deer, she shushed. They were small, canine except for the long legs. They were eating at the seeds in the thick tropical grass in front of them, undisturbed by the human presence.

They should be moving, Timothy said. Like, running away.

Courtney took two steps forward and stamped her feet. The deer looked at her.

They're caught in the headlights of your gaze, said Timothy.

What's that? Are you really quoting right now? she said.

Sure, he lied.

The deer stayed where they were. They watched. I don't like it when you do that, Courtney said.

Do what? Timothy asked.

Order for me, she said. He had, when the waiter from Hungary had come to their table surprisingly quickly.

He tried to put his arm around her, but she shrugged him off. Come on, he said.

No, she said.

She walked to the edge of the water, which was the bay. The beach was on the other side of the island. The hotel had been built here a hundred years ago, by J. P. Morgan and Joseph Pulitzer and Henry Goodyear and all the rest. They pretended to be duck hunting, but they were doing the things that millionaires did. They put the hotel on this side for ease of getting the building materials across the water, barged over from mainland Georgia. It had been in the guidebook that Courtney read on the drive down from Brooklyn. Courtney had woken up one morning and said, after they took their morning walk around the oval at Marine Park, I have to get out of here. The oval was sad concrete. The grass inside was tan and old. A block away they walked past the PTSD firemen outside the Mariners Inn. For a long time they'd been doing just the same thing. They found ways to get a week's vacation. Timothy wouldn't let her drive until they were well into Maryland. They didn't talk on car rides anymore, like they had when they first started dating, five years before—even when they couldn't find a radio station. For a while Courtney talked to her parents on her cell phone. Timothy felt that he knew them almost as well as he knew his own. He hadn't stopped for a bathroom break until D.C.

The two of them looked out at the bay, where there was one red light blinking: a lighthouse. Timothy, rebuffed in his advances, settled for leaning backward on the railing so he could look half at her and half at the old hotel.

It's creepy out here, he said.

I don't think it is, she said. She had picked the place after hearing her coworker talk about it in a hushed voice on her office phone. More than romantic, the coworker had whispered. Southern. Timothy was convinced when she promised him there would be opportunities to swim, his largest indicator of a vacation.

Well, it is, he said, brushing a no-see-um off his chest. There's no people around. It's like there's a curfew or something.

It seemed to Timothy that this bothered Courtney.

Why would there be a curfew? she said.

I don't know, maybe it was in the fine print somewhere, he said. Half off the hotel reservations and free dinners as long as you're in by ten.

But that doesn't even make sense, she said.

Maybe it's because of those wolves we just saw.

They were deer, Tim!

Maybe these are bloodsucking deer.

Courtney angled her body into Timothy. Bloodsucking deer! she fake squealed.

You never know in these places, he said. You just can't tell.

They watched the lighthouse blink red and dark for a while. Timothy stroked Courtney's shoulder. She didn't pull away.

Maybe the vampire deer are owned by the hotel, Courtney said, her breath in his ear. Maybe it's all a setup.

I bet the valets are in on the whole thing, Timothy whispered. That's why they keep hopping into those go-carts—to let the deer out from their cages.

Courtney giggled. Timothy pressed on. By day, he said in his movie-announcer voice, they feed them the carcasses of dead guests, and once it gets dark, they go loose.

Courtney turned in toward Timothy and held each of his jacket lapels in her hands. She pushed her forehead into his chest. Save me, Tim, save me! she shouted.

He felt something triumphant. There was a heaviness in his throat. Maybe this trip would make him better at this. He was running out of ideas. He said, That's my job.

He knew it was the wrong thing to say once her forehead stopped kneading his chest.

What the hell's that supposed to mean? she said.

From the bloodsucking deer, he added.

She let go of his neck. For a while they leaned against the railing next to each other. Timothy waited for something to happen.

Aren't you going to say something? Courtney said.

I don't really know what the problem is, Timothy said. Courtney started walking back to the hotel.

Jesus, Courtney, he said.

I want to go home, she said.

Courtney, come on, he said again. She didn't answer.

She walked the long slow curved lamp-lit path toward the hotel porch. There were plants hanging off the rafters, green overgrown ones, their pots sprinkled with dried-out petals and swaying in the dead air. She ignored the valet who tipped his cap at her and said, Evening ma'am. She planted herself on one of the white rocking chairs and sat in it, motionless, her face in her hands.

When eventually she spread her fingers apart and looked through them, to see what the night looked like, the valet was leaning against the railing with his back to her. His khaki shorts, she noticed, had the symbol of the hotel printed on them in white, on the side. He was wearing a white polo shirt, which was tucked into his pants. She imagined that this was emblazoned with the hotel signature too. It was only his belt that was something different, a pattern of red lobsters in a blue sea. Timothy always complained that she paid too much attention to little things. She never found a way to tell him that because he didn't, he wouldn't understand.

The valet stayed with his arms on his hips, looking out toward the path for cars coming in. After a while he said, I'm sure you didn't mean to be rude.

Courtney arched her shoulders.

Excuse me? she said.

Rude, he said. You know, when you don't respond to something that someone says to you.

Courtney had that feeling that the human body secretes when it starts panicking, though it's in no immediate danger. She started to open her mouth, then thought better of it.

Go on, the valet said. I can take it. But she pushed her hackles down, and the panicked feeling began to subside.

I see people like you fellas all the time, the valet said. Courtney wondered how old he might be. This hotel isn't getting any newer. And northerners don't tip, you know.

Is that true? Courtney said. That's not true for us. My boyfriend tipped you when we left yesterday.

The valet raised his eyebrows. Boyfriend? he said. Aren't you a little old for that?

Courtney thought she would feel the panicked feeling again, but she didn't. Who even knows, she said.

The valet squinted lazily out onto the lawn, toward the dock. He pointed his thumb at the chair Courtney was sitting in, and said, You're sitting right where Sean Penn was sitting.

Really? Courtney said.

Yep, he said. Last Christmas. Big Christmas party. The heat wasn't working in the ballroom, so they put outdoor heaters into a tent out here, and there must have been a thousand people.

Good business, Courtney said.

Good tips, the valet said. When I got Sean Penn's car, once he got in, he gave me five hundred dollars.

A good day, Courtney said.

The valet nodded. He was drunk, said the valet. But he was real friendly. He shook my hand. The valet showed her his palm, as if the touch were still there. Are you some kind of actress too? he said.

Courtney thought about the nonprofit where she worked. It helped set up typing classes for women and the handicapped in Kibera, and got them work digitizing documents. She had wanted a women's issue job, but she wasn't in love with the outsourcing. Sometimes she left that part out. Timothy was an air conditioner repairman at an apartment complex in midtown, and he made more money than she did. Yes, she told the valet. My husband too.

Husband? the valet said.

You know what I mean.

I guess so. Sometimes you have to try it out. Would I have seen any of your movies?

I doubt it, she told him. She suddenly felt very tired. She realized, without having anything she could do about it, that she didn't have any dollar bills in her purse. The drink was draining from her body, and she would have been ready for Timothy to walk over to her, for her to say she was sorry, for him to apologize first. I know you do things your own way, he would say, fumbling. They could make arguments out of nothing. It was exhausting just thinking about it.

The valet looked carefully down the wide sweep of the road, buzzing with night bugs.

Hell, he said, there's no one coming. It's the off-season, he said. He sat in the wicker chair next to her.

They listened to the creaking of the old windows, above their heads.

Have you ever been to Disney World? the valet asked. When she didn't answer immediately, he said, Lots of guests go there from here.

No, she said. Timothy had gone all the time when he was younger, with his family, she thought she remembered.

The valet didn't look surprised. For a while, he said, I used to work at one of the hotels right on the Disney campus. All-Star Sports Resort—although I liked Movies better. Sometimes they let us transfer. It wasn't so up-class as it is here, but I liked it.

Courtney continued looking out over the porch.

I had a friend there, the valet said, whose job was to be one of the walk-around characters. One night it was such a long day, around the Christmas holidays, that after the parade, when he finally got off work, he wore his costume directly to the restaurant we were meeting at in Downtown Disney—he was one of those monsters from *Monsters, Inc.* At the place, he kept the mask from the costume between his legs next to a bar stool, but he stayed in the costume all night. And when parents came out of the restaurant with their kids—who I'd think should have been in bed by that time of night, but the guests always try to get as much in as they can—they'd cover their kids' eyes when they walked past me and my friend. Like, seven or eight times. It wasn't a coincidence.

Courtney had started paying attention in the middle of the story. The scene appeared in front of her above the porch railing. She realized that she was almost crying. She felt the tears coming up, like an epiphany or a revelation, which would clear her head and make everything sensible then; help her order her more or less acceptable life, she thought levelheadedly, an all right life even though it seemed problematic then. Was he all right, your friend? Courtney said, but the valet took it the wrong way.

I can put you in touch with him, if you're looking for some acting work, he said gently.

Courtney gave him a tight smile, and nothing else.

On the wharf Timothy turned back around again, looked away from the hotel, looked out on the lighthouse blinking red, and off, and red, and off. He was too old to be jealous of someone talking to Courtney. He concentrated on a docked fishing boat whose cabin was covered with Christmas lights, not plugged in. It wasn't like that when they met. It was at the Mariners, on Fillmore, where Timothy was watching a Rangers game with his lovesick cousin Eamon. Eamon lived in Carroll Gardens then, off the F train, but he came back to the Mariners sometimes since his girlfriend left. The whole bar noticed Courtney when she walked in. For some reason she came right up to Timothy. Hi, she'd said. Let's talk for a little while. He wanted to tell her that he didn't usually go to the Mariners; there was just the Rangers game. For the rest of the time there he tried to explain that. It had been a hot night, like this one, when they walked outside of the bar, leaving Eamon behind. It was muggy. Fillmore was the same distance from the water as here, practically, if Timothy thought about it geographically.

They had reservations at this hotel for three more nights. They were staying in the annex. It was a fifteen-minute drive away, and they would be here until the end of the week. Then there was nothing else. He guessed they would drive back home. They still rented their condo. He was OK with that, didn't itch for anything different, which was why Courtney called him a fool, off and on again. There was all the time in the world, though. The water confirmed: all the time in the world. Timothy stayed at the end of the wharf for a while, waiting for Courtney to come back, but she didn't, and at a certain point he didn't dare turn around and look for her. It would have admitted defeat.

He looked out over the water. In the reflection of the lamplight, and the intermittent glow of the lighthouse, the bay between the island and the land shimmered, just a few lights on the other side of the coast. Timothy thought he saw something surfacing and disappearing in the waves, and when he looked closely he was sure he saw something, and heard a corresponding animal sound to go with it, but then he couldn't be sure it wasn't driftwood. The water lapped and lapped.

He walked down the end of the wharf to the dock, which had a door over it, a chain-link door leading to nowhere, with triangular extensions on either side, like sails or ears, to prevent climbing around. Timothy did it anyway, swinging himself around the sail. He walked to the end of the dock, where all the lights died away.

No one called for him. Courtney was on the porch. The seafood restaurant built on pilings right off the shore was closed, or else nobody was out to bother him at this hour. No waiters or valets came running. He'd always wanted to do something unaccustomed in life, like jump into an open body of water with all his clothes on, his shoes even. He thought about this sometimes on planes coming into JFK for a landing, over Rockaway Beach. But as he knew he would, he took off his clothes methodically, his jacket first and then his shirt, waiting modestly for his jeans to be last, his best pair of dress jeans. He laid these all out on the edge of the wooden dock. When he fell backward into the water, it hardly felt cold; just a continuation of the air on his skin. He remembered, without meaning to, what it had felt like, as a child, to learn how to swim—the overchlorinated high school pool, the gray lockers off the gym, the bang of their swinging back and forth. He dove deep, resurfaced, realized he couldn't see the bottom, or anything close to the bottom, and for the first time in many times of swimming he felt scared, unsure of what was below the surface. Inadvertently he touched some driftwood, pulled his hand back in shock. It was so black, as far as he could see, and he couldn't lift himself up farther. The oily water opened around him like a mouth, the orifice as far as he could see of some face. He scrambled up the slimy old metal rungs of the dock ladder. He sat there on the edge, gasping for breath, though he hadn't realized he'd needed to. The hot air dried him after a while, and slowly his breathing calmed. He was shivering, leaning back, his arms hugging what they could of his body, and he felt entirely satiated.

TO LIVE IN THE PRESENT

MOMENT IS A MIRACLE

This was when Hayden was living in graduate housing at Brandeis. He had a little room to himself and his own door with a lock on it, and he never put posters up. This was during the period of us-learning-to-be-better-communicators, which was something he felt strongly about.

Hayden had become good at talking about his feelings, even though that was something we hadn't done when we were first friends. He broke his wrist and was in a cast before high school and I helped him with that, but it doesn't count. I didn't talk about feelings with anyone, because Lorris was too young. Hayden lost his virginity to his girlfriend at the same time I did with mine, and we didn't talk about it until two months after. And even then I didn't bring it up, just said, *me too*, after he said his piece—I've got something to tell you, man. That was in the stands at Icahn Stadium in the spring, right after Hayden got knocked out of medaling at Cities in the 800-meter run. I'd done the mile, and broke 4:40 for the first time. He had long hair that season, and he was beginning to lose interest in track because of his girlfriend. A few months ago something incredible happened, he said.

They called the place where Hayden lived Grad, capital *G*, as if it were more than a place but also a state of mind. It was far from the rest of the dormitories and classroom buildings: the main campus was up a winding road at the top of a hill, where there was a corny little castle that someone had built in the 1950s. The type of thing that, at nighttime, looked amazing, lit up with red ramparts and a view of the Charles and the train tracks at the bottom of the hill. But in the daytime it looked like something that someone had built in the 1950s.

Hayden was happy to be living in Grad, as a junior, even though everyone gave him a hard time for it: complaining that it was too far away and that they never saw him anymore, because he always retreated there to his single room and the graduate students with their guitars, reading theory in their beds. He maintained that this wasn't true; that he, for instance, spent a lot of time in the Peace Room, which was in the place where the dungeon would be if the castle had a dungeon. He took me there once, although he opened the door first and peeked in to make sure no one was inside, because he said that the Peace Room regulars usually didn't like to be disturbed. Not that I was a disturbance at all, he said. I was a good influence on him, and he thanked me for that.

I'd always wanted to go to school away from home, but sometimes things don't work perfectly. CUNY takes just about anyone, and they promised they'd be opening dorms at Brooklyn College by my sophomore year. They didn't, of course. Brooklyn College is the type of place that hasn't changed since my parents went there—my dad on the GI Bill, my mother looking for a husband who wasn't Italian—and they didn't end up finishing those dorms just like they never built the swimming pool that my dad and his Navy friends were always asking for. What were they supposed to do to stay in shape? they asked the administration. The provost at the time was a running guru who had done Boston, New York, and Berlin, enough years after that other war, and he tried to get them to start a track team (they didn't), or at least go for runs with him all around Brooklyn. They did it once, but what they really wanted was to hit something or be completely covered by water, and running was a pretty poor exchange. I ended up living at home and saving my money, listening to my dad snicker about Brooklyn College. He'd stopped taking classes his senior year, and there wasn't really an explanation why. Some things just happen. It was a better experience for my mother. If I could stand to, I stayed at the Sugar Bowl after classes until dinner, avoiding watching Lorris get back from school and sit right down to his homework. Eventually I stayed longer and longer, even when I wasn't taking classes, looking at the captioned TV. I established once that the waitress knew my dad when he used to hang out there. After that she gave me the stale bagels, which I'd take home and let him eat.

Hayden was always trying to get me to come visit, and I did, more often than I should have. Academically, there hadn't been much of a difference between him and me, though I guess he wrote better essays. My mother said she didn't think it was worth it to go away to expensive private colleges when we had perfectly good ones here. We do, and what's the difference in the end, but Hayden seemed to enjoy living away. He said, even up to junior year, people had late-night conversations about the things they were studying, the books that classes assigned. Which sounds like bullshit to me, like one of the brochures that the private colleges send from random places in the South. Nobody was that earnest about it at Brooklyn, though if you kept your head down you could get an education. I was taking my math requirement that semester, even though the professor asked if I was sure I wanted to. I'd been in and out. He said, Are you staying this time? I said I was back for good. It was a survey: "Mathematical Topics." Sometimes you learn some good things.

I promised myself I wouldn't spend more than two weekends a month up at Hayden's that year—though because he was a junior, I was starting to get anxious that I was losing the chance. When we talked about it, he said simply, Literally, whenever. He invited Lorris too, though it was mostly just to be nice. He said we could move a mattress in and he could get me someone's old Brandeis ID and a copy of his key. I did end up getting a copy of the key, for the nights when Hayden went off with a girl, although those were very rare: because when I was there, he said that it was more important that we spend time together, and catch up; girls would be around forever.

Hayden had taken a class last semester that he said had changed his life. He had started out majoring in business, like his father wanted. His dad studied econ and law in Tel Aviv and was a real estate broker here. But the class, called "Peace, Social Change, and a New Way of Viewing Human Interrelations," made Hayden switch to sociology. You'd think those would have been difficult, stressful times for him, full of calls home and imploring his mother for support, but Hayden rarely called home, and actually didn't know too much about how his parents were doing—just like they didn't see much of him besides the semester's bill, which they immediately sent up to Hayden. Even I asked if it would be tough to graduate on time with requirements, and he said, Please. It's Brandeis.

"Peace, Social Change, Etc." was a class taught by an elderly Iranian man named Yahya, who had converted to Judaism twenty-five years ago. He was one of a whole new host of Brandeis professors who were beginning to wear jackets without ties, and in the winter, under his blazer, a blue turtleneck that had sweat stains seeping from under the arms. You had to write multiple essays to get into the class, and it was only the most talented and dedicated who did—everyone wanted a spot because every other week they went on peace retreats to one of Yahya's numerous friends' cabins, in the Berkshires, or on the North Shore, or near Walden Pond. There, they cooked meals for each other, drank pinot grigio with Yahya, and practiced looking into each other's eyes when they conversed, while they listed one thing they appreciated about each and every member of the class. Yahya wouldn't smoke with them, but he said that it wasn't for him to set rules for them to go by, and when, on the first day of class, they put smoking pot into the legal section of their new social constitution, he said that this would be a good experiment in learning each other's boundaries.

This was after their trip to the Berkshires, and I was staying until Monday. Hayden was sitting at his desk, mixing songs on GarageBand, and I was lying on the mattress, trying to decide why it somehow worked that Hayden left all the walls blank in his room. Above his desk he had a quote—"We are very good at preparing to live, but not very good at living"—but that was it, with his computer and the wires of his speakers in a corner. It was barely ten when three of his friends came over, bringing with them their leftover dinner, which we ate on the floor, the new people sitting on the mattress and Hayden in his chair. He offered them a beer but passed on one himself. He had told me that he was beginning to feel that he had a small drinking problem and had made me promise that I wouldn't let him black out that night. He had a habit of doing so, back home when we'd go to bars in the East Village.

One of the girls got a text on her phone to say there was something going on in Gordon, which was a fifteen-minute walk away and just outside the main entrance to campus. There was a semifamous DJ playing there who had been making the rounds of New England colleges. The walk was frigid, and when we arrived we found only six guys from the tennis team drinking pink champagne out of a bottle. They were sitting in a circle and passing the bottle to one another. Hayden seemed to know a few of them, and I was introduced, and we let the bottle go around maybe once or twice before it was empty. The tennis players were reminiscing about stories from their preseason camp, and Hayden was listening politely and asking clarifying questions here and there. For a while we passed around the empty bottle, taking a swig from it, as if there was some left at the bottom. There didn't seem to be any more bottles, or any newcomers, so we left.

There was a similar situation in the works at a frat house, and this was promised to be better. Hayden had met his last girlfriend at a frat house. We had been slotted next on the beer pong table, and he told me to wait a second, he had to run to the bathroom. I never felt so alone as when he disappeared while I was visiting at Brandeis. Everyone, the entire time, knew that I wasn't supposed to be around. The time he met his girlfriend he had disappeared, and when he came back, it was with two girls, one obviously his interest and one dragged along for my sake. That one, Gloria, had a perfectly diamond-shaped scar on her lower back. I traced the parallel lines later that night, in one of the upstairs rooms at the frat, once Hayden had brought his girl home. That lasted almost all semester, but she'd ended it after the Peace class started and he asked her to keep her eyes open during sex.

The frat party was in the basement, below a set of water-heating pipes, and every once in a while a particularly tall boy wearing a backward flat-brim cap would hit his head on the ceiling. We made our way over to the bar area to get drinks. Hayden gripped my outside shoulder and pulled my ear close.

Play along, he said.

We were next in line when Hayden started collecting cups and bottles and making two drinks himself, with the bartender frowning over him. One of the backward-hat kids stopped dancing and came over.

What's up, big guy? he said.

Making myself a drink, and one for Bob Dylan's grandson here. Backward-hat looked at me and then put a hand on the edge of the cup.

This is for Bob Dylan's grandson? he said.

That's right, said Hayden. This is him right here. We shook hands, his fingers clammy with sweat. He's doing front work before his grandpa's last concert, he said. Backward-cap nodded. Dylan's doing something big this time, Hayden added. It's a multivisual, audience-participation, varied-media project. He put his hand on my shoulder again.

It's called Project W, I said. Opens at House of Blues.

Backward-cap opened his eyes wide. Well, it's really great to have you here. Anything you need.

We'll keep you posted, Hayden said, as we walked toward the dance floor.

I never like dancing with a cup in my hand, but Hayden was a natural. It became just another appendage to his gyration. He told me once in that new phase of being completely open that the dance floor scared him, that he felt that there were fish-strings going from the place where his neck meets the back of his head, out to his various responsibilities: me (was I having fun?), the girl from class who had put her hand on his arm outside, other hangers-on. It was almost too much to think about while trying to look passable. But he made it look easy, and if he hadn't said it I never would have known. He was always doing interesting things with his arms in time to the music, mixing it up, keeping it light.

The friend from earlier who had brought leftover dinner had materialized here, and she was doing her best to edge closer and closer to Hayden. She'd told us earlier in the night that she didn't drink but smoked weed on Shabbat, as long as someone else lit it for her. Religious, Hayden whispered in my ear, with his eyes going up and down.

I could appreciate that she was making an effort, and I started to look around to see if there was anyone else I'd met before whom I could tag along with while they danced. Hayden was premiering for the night a toothbrushing move I'd seen him pull off to great success before. She mimicked the motion and stayed in sync with Hayden's twists, and got one hand on his hand, and twirled herself around.

They had both hands together now, and he was leading her in a sort of fake fox-trot even though the music was reggaeton, and she was laughing at the antics. I was pretending to be doing the same without a partner, so I was close enough to hear her say, leaning in, Let's go back to Grad.

Hayden cocked his head sideways and then he said, Look, really drawn out. He was making perfect eye contact with her and still holding her hands. He kept holding them for what seemed like a moment too long, like he was a child again and he was waiting for one of our parents or teachers to tell him what to do. This was fun and I'd love to dance with you again some other time, but to-night I can't, he said.

Then he patted her forearm and turned toward me and signaled the door.

It was snowing softly outside, but the wind with the snow on the ground was making sheet-fingers over the layer of frost. We crossed a street where I remember Hayden had told me about one time when he and a girl had kissed for fifteen minutes on the double yellow line. Cars went past them on both sides, but because the two of them were in the middle they never got close.

I remember once Hayden told me that he was finding it difficult to live in the moment, and that he thought this was the major problem in his life from which everything else stemmed. Hanging out with me, he said, he was always thinking about the next time I'd be able to come up. When meditating (he'd started meditating), he could only think about texts waiting on the phone in his pocket. He felt that if there were some way to narrow in, appreciate some type of now, he would be cured. It was a Heisenberg uncertainty issue, which the "Mathematical Topics" professor was always ragging on: only being able to know position or momentum. Physically, if you tried to measure either, you'd be pushing it just a little bit. The professor put red marks all over that on a test. *Close*, he wrote. *Good to think about this.*

It seemed like Hayden was going to bring something like that up again. There was a straightening of his posture that came when he was about to say something important. But instead he asked if I wouldn't mind walking through the cemetery instead of going to find another party. He said it was absurdly beautiful at night—he used the word *beautiful*; I don't think I'd ever heard someone use that word out loud before—and he liked to walk on the gravel path.

We were leaning against a pedestal, TAYMAN, JAMES—1927, off the path, out of the wind. Hayden said, You know, I've thought about kissing you, but I don't think that would make me happy either.

I asked what he meant.

He straightened his back and raised his head, and then he slumped back down lower on the rock.

It sounds a little like something, but that's not the way it really was in my head, he said.

I'm sure.

It's just something I said.

Yeah, yeah, I said.

He tapped his finger against the *T* in Tayman, and I watched the dirt get under his fingernail. His nail and the rock made a dry clink, again and again.

Then he said, Let's try something. He jumped up. Let's be spontaneous, he said.

What do you want to do? I asked.

He told me, and we ran down the hill—toward the Charles, frozen there on the bottom.

It was close. He was ahead of me. There were the train tracks; up at the top of the little mountain the castle was blinking, an antenna hovering up above, some of the windows lit, full of the warmth of other people, their books and lights and extra sweatshirts. Hayden got to the edge of the ice first, and he rolled up one sleeve and threw a big rock from the bank out toward the middle, and it bounced. There was a cracking sound, as if something live was coming up from the bottom. But he was already at the center, and I started running to catch up, and I've always felt that you run faster at night, that you're counting the lampposts, or the trees, or the number of man-made objects stuck in the ice flow, as if to say that we have been here. We must have run for miles, Hayden half a pace in front of me in that perfect form he had, dodging islands and branches and large objects in the dark.

It was a cold winter. Fall came late, winter early. It snowed a little, but mostly it was just cold. You could run on rivers like that, without any problem, the dry ice tractioning your feet. The air bit the back of your throat. The surface was always solid. The skin on your fingers got dry and white. The ice cracks in the night sounded like conversation.

CLEAN

The first one of them to get herpes was Desmond. He was at NYU graduate school at the time, studying microbiology, and they offered him a free room in the grad student cabins on the Sterling Forest upstate campus for a semester. He didn't have much money. His dad wasn't getting the same amount of plumbing work as he used to. He took it, and moved out of Brooklyn, for the first and last time, and sequestered himself in the woods near Woodstock, which he'd always wanted to get to but never had the chance.

Those were long winter nights. The skiing was good, and cheap, in Sterling Forest. It's only an hour north of the city. But nobody much knows about it. Desmond taught himself how to ski that season. One evening, right as it was getting dark, he dislocated his thumb sticking his hand into the hard snow for balance, and had to go to the office for a first-aid kit. The woman working there was warm and gave him hot chocolate. She told him to make himself comfortable, and he did. He stayed on the couch while she changed radio stations, looking for the Rangers game. Later, when they went to his cabin, he had almost forgotten what it was like to love a woman. He came quickly, embarrassingly, hot and sweaty under the polyester sheets. She left to drive to her house in the dark, and he didn't offer to take her; and he never called again. In two weeks he started getting cold sores. Perhaps it hadn't been her, but he always assumed.

This was the seventies. Nobody cared too much about a bit of abnormal skin. And it was on his face. It seemed more like a chronic but unimportant dermatological problem. Desmond tried not to think so much about it. He went through a sexual revelation after getting back from Sterling Forest. His crowd liked to go out to Staten Island, where the bouncers let you in without the best clothing, and the girls were Italian and loose. Desmond and his best friend, Harlan, would borrow the car of their friend Perry, who was gay, and they'd drive down the Belt Parkway over the Verrazano together. Perry's scene was more in Manhattan, but he kept the car because his father gave it to him. His roommate, Carol, used it to drive to the beach. Desmond and Harlan would pick up the car from Perry's apartment, pat him on the shoulder, and fly over the bridge. Desmond entertained Harlan on the ride with stories from his semester upstate. Harlan had never been farther north than Van Cortlandt Park. While Desmond drove the candy-red Mustang, the windows down, the radio on 104.3, Harlan curled in the passenger seat and complained about finding true love. Yeah, Desmond said, but why say the truth about it?

It was on Staten Island where they first met Ida, who had perpetual thick-rimmed glasses. They had noticed her a few times before they formally met, because she was known to stand on the bar at that particular place every Saturday just as it turned midnight, and slowly take off the turtleneck sweaters she liked to wear. One night Desmond pushed forward and put a hand up to help her back onto the dance floor, and instead of taking his hand she jumped down and pushed her finger on his lips. By the time they left they had already kissed backed up next to the jukebox, so when Desmond got the keys from Harlan and took her back to the

Mustang he knew they'd be going further. She pulled her pants down herself but wouldn't help him with his. He suddenly felt shy about it. So he did what he could with his mouth and she seemed to enjoy it, because eventually she unbuttoned his fly and blew him while he leaned back, every so often, on the horn.

Ida's herpes was much worse than Desmond's, and though she was certain it was from him, she never said anything about it. She wasn't the type of girl who was involved with many men, and the turtleneck stunt was something she'd seen a cousin of hers do. She'd had a serious boyfriend in Vietnam who, before he left, had taught her all about sex. They did it everywhere he could imagine, and, eventually, some of the places she tentatively suggested. Can it be standing up somewhere? she said. Girl, he said, how come you're so naive? When he came back with chlamydia and was good enough to tell her about it beforehand, she broke it off. She felt somewhat guilty. She'd been looking for a good time ever since. The ex-boyfriend only called on the phone, from Montana, where he was living.

The blisters that she got, every few weeks, on the inner upper part of her thighs, turned pink after a day. There were worse diseases, and Ida knew this. Grand scheme, what she had didn't compare. Even still, it hurt to walk when the blisters were in full. On the second day they would begin to stream pus. A day later they scabbed over. She learned the schedule quickly enough, but worse was the uncertainty. Doctors didn't know what it was, but they advised that she inform everyone whom she would potentially be having sex with. They were fairly sure, they said, that it couldn't be transmitted between outbreaks. They asked questions about her habits, shook their heads. She began to police her body, so strictly that sometimes she'd step out of film lectures at the New School to go to the bathroom and take a look. In the stalls with no locks, so that she had to hold the door shut with one hand, she kept her head down, watching her legs. The panic seemed to rise from them, from below her toes, and by the time it seeped up to her head she'd have to let go of the door and clutch her arms around her chest.

One Saturday, after having gotten only three hours of sleep the night before, she got drunk too quickly. These things aren't anybody's fault. She had been at Two Fish Bar with Desmond and Harlan again, and, as they'd become accustomed to doing, they came stumbling out the wooden doorway onto Father Capodanno Boulevard walking toward the real clubs, closer to the bad end of the island. They passed the red Mustang parked at a smashed meter. Ida kept tripping, and Desmond was ignoring her, so it fell to Harlan to guide her with his arm. She kept adjusting her pant legs. By the end of the boulevard they had gotten fairly close. Desmond went inside, and ordered his own drink, but Ida and Harlan walked back to the Mustang, and they had unprotected sex. How do you feel about me? Harlan said. Ida pushed him out in time.

Harlan's experience with herpes began with a hard day at work. He had a job as a stringer for the New York office of the *Washington Post*, and because there was so much crime in New York in those days, the paper had a full office. Washingtonians loved reading about how unclean New York was. It was the only thing that people responded positively to in readership surveys. New York was a mess. Harlan himself had gotten mugged three times in the past month, so that he'd taken to taping a five-dollar bill under his sock, only a dollar or two in his wallet. The annoying part was the trip to the DMV for a new license. He needed the license because he drove in to work, Brooklyn to the city, and it was one day on the drive that he started feeling particularly under the weather. He trudged the stairs up to the eighth floor because the elevator was broken again.

In the office for three days straight he wrote crime copy with a 102-degree fever. It came in bursts with the chills, so that he couldn't turn the fan off fast enough to get the heavy woolen blanket he'd taken to stowing under his chair. He went to the doctor, who gave him ibuprofen and asked if he'd been to Europe recently, or a farm, and didn't understand anything until he got the blisters on his penis. One doctor misdiagnosed it as a ruptured birthmark, but the infectious disease unit at Maimonides knew better. Even stringers at the *Post* had health insurance. He won a Scripps Award for a series he was working on during that time, but his head wasn't in it.

Harlan reacted by looking for someone to blame. He never talked about it openly, and it began to eat away at his chest from the inside. He made little whimpering noises at his desk when the typewriter broke. He never asked Desmond about it. Desmond was cold for a few weeks after the Ida-car situation. Harlan hadn't considered Ida a possibility. They hardly knew each other. He formed the mistaken idea that he got it from an ex-girlfriend who'd recently come out of the closet, and he began to feel disgusted by the idea of gay sex. He used the word *faggot* indiscriminately. Still, he went to work every day.

He began to play out imagined situations in his head. He didn't like the idea of having sex with someone without telling them about it. He also wasn't very good at talking to people. It was the only thing holding him back as a reporter, though he wrote good copy. If he couldn't tell anyone and he didn't have sex, then he couldn't get married. No marriage, no kids, no grandkids, getting old alone. He'd be like his uncle Vance, who called on the phone every Friday. The call came at the same time every week. It was a before-dinner call. Just checking in, his uncle Vance would say. And he'd say good-bye: Good to talk.

One afternoon Perry called Harlan at his office. He told him that he wanted to get a drink together. Harlan assumed that it was something about his recent behavior and the slurs. He was indignant, then embarrassed. He left his coat on the rack on the way out.

At the bar, in Greenwich Village, at the place where West Fourth Street meets West Twelfth, a nightmare of geometry, they sat in the dark back and drank McSorley's beer brewed in a basement nearby. Perry and Harlan had been drinking it since they were kids, taking the train in from Bensonhurst. It had an aftertaste, like candy, that they'd never found anywhere else. Harlan used to put a piece of bread in his pocket before going out, when they were in high school, and eat it before sneaking back into the dark house, to mask the smell. Italian bread was the only thing that could do it. After four beers Perry put a hand on his leg. Harlan left it there for a minute, and then angled away. After another beer Perry put his hand on the other leg, and Harlan left it. In the small bathroom, with graffiti on the walls, Perry leaned down and unbuttoned his pants, and Harlan put his hands through Perry's long hair.

At first Perry decided that he'd go on with his usual life. That it was his right—this wasn't a Scarlet Letter—to do what he wanted as long as he wasn't endangering anyone else. No one died from herpes. Then, after weeks of no communication from Harlan, in the moment after he told a strange man about it while they walked out of a bar in Bay Ridge to hail a taxi to his home, he realized his mistake. The look on the man's face did it. It's what? he said. Blotches appeared on his face. He took the cab himself and the cab screamed away. Perry sat on the curb. Then he walked home. He decided to put sex out of his mind until he could think of a better option. Still, he couldn't escape it entirely. One morning after not enough sleep, staying awake walking the night streets, he emerged from the shower and, without paying attention, took his roommate Carol's towel. He rubbed it all over his body, trying to get clean; the way the steam gets under pores, as if something has been forgotten. Jumping into a pile of autumn leaves as a young boy, the tongue of a first kiss, the particular light from a dying lightbulb in the ceiling of that room, his voice whispering, Maybe. He rubbed and he rubbed. He didn't realize it was her towel until she was already in the shower, and by then he didn't want to knock or make excuses. Besides, the thing couldn't be that transmittable.

Within months, Carol was displaying symptoms that she mistook for mosquito bites. She was new to the city. She came from Michigan. She had grown up on a horse farm. She had always wanted to be a milkmaid princess, and then, in high school, a theater star. She hawked tickets to comedy clubs late nights, to make the money for auditions. She didn't tell her parents about it. She read plays over breakfast, walked the lonely morning streets with coffee, went to see anything avant-garde, tentatively liked the Living Theatre. She'd never had sex before. She assumed that it would be like a thunderclap. She had the low-grade symptom kind, and she didn't know until after she was married, to a good man who moved them to Suffolk County, where she taught drama in the junior high school. He had words for her. They thought about getting a divorce. They slept for many months afterward with their backs to each other, until one day the husband turned over. She looked at him over her shoulder with something resembling desire. Fuck it, he said.

SHATTER THE TREES AND
BLOW THEM AWAY

t was 1944 and they told us to take the overnight to Jemez Springs, New Mexico, and when I said, Where's that? the guy at the ticket counter at Grand Central train station said, Middle a bumfuck nowhere, that's what I know, and the guy in the conductor's cap next to him said, Why all the one-way tickets to Los Alamos lately, and I said, Some things are classified for a reason. I was gone.

Lise was in the aisle across from me as we passed into the tunnel, and I saw her reading *The Science of Mechanics*. When she saw that I didn't get off in Chicago like everyone else, she asked if I was by chance a man of science, and I told her engineering. She did particle physics, and already we were sharing a secret.

The compound was built on the site of what used to be an all-boys school. They had a bit of a library, but now the Army Corps was underneath it, building a particle accelerator. Everything was claptrap—the wooden sidings, the paint above the windows. My room didn't even have a shower, although hers did, and I begged her to let me use it, an excuse to be close by, her roommate yelling from her bedroom when I tramped back in, Is he here again?

Everyone spent all day at work. You can't understand it. Somebody had come to each of us, put a pointer finger in the center of our chests, and said, Serve your country. We who were too scared for infantry, and spent all our post-finals beer money worrying if we'd lose our draft-exempt status. But they said, make us the Gadget, and everything will change.

I thought Lise and I would be the youngest, but graduate students were like leaves. All the professors who had been disappearing from class, or the Institute higher-ups who had become conspicuously absent, were showing up here, from Berkeley, Cambridge, Ann Arbor. There were mathematicians, theoretical physicists, chemists who knew all about fission, armaments engineers flown in from Normandy and their college buddies from MIT. There was no one else from Brooklyn College.

It was summer camp surrounded by barbed-wire fences. There was only the one cantina in the neighboring town and it was packed with shirt-tucked-in scientists trying to talk to the locals. It was always a male crowd. The women were something special, in their studies—they tended to be better than the rest of us—and their small number. Men danced with each other in order to keep dances alive. I was lucky to meet her on the train, I told her once. She rolled her eyes and said, Whatever that means.

Meanwhile, I was busier than I'd ever been in my life. I used to imagine making whole flying cities when I was a kid, designing just the tallest pinpoint towers and letting the lessers take care of the rest, according to my dashed-off plans. My father tuh'd, as if he'd seen it before, and didn't say anything else. In high school I made bottle rockets and Roman candles, and then the college gave me an aerodynamics lab, and they brought me to the compound to work on how the Gadget would fall. The third day there, after I sat in on theory meetings and filled four notebooks, I spent all afternoon doing exploded view drawings—from right to left: the nose casing, the uranium target, the uranium bullet that would set it off, and the explosive on the back end, which mattered most for me. The explosive had to be triggered somewhere before it landed, or half the power would go into the ground. We had to know the drop path and design the casing so the explosive could go off at the right time. Four days later when I had a mock-up, they gave me an assistant from Texas Tech, and together we started dropping models off the top of dormitory buildings. Then the explosives engineers redesigned the bullet, and we had to redesign the casing, and it was back to square one.

Lise had an office all to herself at the far end of the compound. The guy next to her was also in particles and kept a carton of cookies on his desk. He was one of the last holdovers who didn't believe in special relativity, but he was such a good ideas man that they took him from Minnesota in case something clicked out here in the heat. Lise argued with him all the time in the beginning, but eventually she just stopped by for an oatmeal raisin in the morning and waved when he went out, still busy over numbers.

I had dinner breaks then, and I would go visit once he was gone. Sometimes I kneaded her shoulders while she stared at her graphs. She had this idea that you'd be able to measure the theoretical explosion with entropy calculations. She was spending her time manipulating convergent series. When she wrote integral signs the muscles in her neck twitched.

One of the times with my hands on her shoulders, she stood up, took my hand, led me over to the extra chair, and pulled it over to her plush one. We sat parallel to each other and she leaned into me over the arm of her chair. She had her head turned away, toward the papers on her desk. The small hairs on her arm were visible from this close. Her lip quivered every few seconds, and I watched the smooth skin on her neck. I ran my fingers over her arm and let her hear my breathing get heavy. I didn't move. I didn't do more than that. After three minutes she stood up and said, get out, she had work to do.

I needed her to be with me. I set my watch to the point at lunchtime when she came and met me and hugged hello. I walked down different corridors trying to pass her when she didn't know I'd be there. It was the way you can make yourself sick, and finally I was doodling abstract drawings at my drafting bench, running the .2-inch lead pen up and down in geometric and sinusoidal patterns, putting in circles for her eyes and obtuse angles for her bottom lip.

There were no Lise's at home. Some nights I walked the empty streets for something to do, the dirt roads. In winter the snow piled so high the cars got stuck for days. Nobody ever locked their doors.

My father owned the hardware store. He said that he knew everyone in town; he knew what everyone ate for lunch. Sometimes he made sandwiches in the back room, and gave them out to the laborers or the drunks who hung around the store during the day. They talked about the Dodgers, always the Dodgers, as if they would get to heaven through them, and always the park. The park hung out there gleaming. Not in real life—not anything concrete—but the idea of it, all the promises. City Hall was eight miles away, but everyone read the newspapers. It was a college man had been picked, who won the design competition; a man from Connecticut, who loved walking in the outdoors up and over hills. That's what the papers said. There had been mornings, years ago, when the drunks followed him around as he surveyed the area. He had a long coat, my father remembered. He put up a sign that said MARINE PARK.

My father had a little technical skill, and he ended up doing some of the drawings. We still had them, framed, in the hardware store. The architect's name on the bottom. The paths that the speed rail lines would take, all three of them, to service the park and resort. The parking areas for 28,000 cars. Land reclamation for the Circumferential Parkway, bringing Manhattan as close to here as if we were the ones across the river. Two hundred sixty-four acres of walks. Seventeen acres of tennis courts, 9.6 of farm gardens, flower gardens, 38 planned buildings. My father drew them all. A zoo or menagerie. A stadium seating 100,000. A long canal, the big pool, larger even than the lake in Central Park, chlorinated so people could swim. A tunnel connecting the white-sand waterfront to Flatbush Avenue, where the buses would stop and the trains would have their terminus stations. The nine-mile trip from Manhattan would be part of the amusement. A bathing house, open all year for tubercular children, particularly poor ones, and on weekdays and Saturday mornings children could swim free of charge. The Connecticut man, the one morning he gave a speech, said he was bringing the Olympics here. The 1940 Olympics. This was 1933. The land was crawling with surveyors.

It all didn't happen quickly. The money never came. The war started. We shaved our heads on the side and on the top in Marine fashion. Army recruiters came by on the roads, the only things built, meant to bring people to the park. They said, You can't join the Navy if you've got both your parents. There was only three-hour overnight parking in case of invasion by sea. My father wouldn't move the car, said he wasn't helping Roosevelt. Nights, I watched the artillery demonstrations at Fort Tilden, the tracers coming over the Rockaway Peninsula like fireworks. For a moment they lit up the parkland, where nothing had changed. There were strange people who lived on houseboats in the canals running through the grass. They didn't talk to anyone, and we didn't talk to them. I was starting at Brooklyn. The teachers said that science wins war.

One night, coming home from the college, I found my father in the basement of our house, which he'd dug with his own hands, looking at drawings on his amateur drafting bench, in the corner against the rough wall. The Gerritsen gristmill had burned down that afternoon, and I'd gone to see it happen, because it was the most exciting thing around. He was looking at a scaled model, his pencils not in his hand but lying on the other side of the desk: a drawing of the main baseball diamond, with stands on two sides, the ground beveled and the dirt new. We could have had the Dodgers, he was saying, when he looked up. The World Series. We couldn't even get that. He didn't address me often. His lips puckered in a pathetic way. I went over to the desk, picked up one of the pencils, shaded a white line of chalk running down the base lines to the outfield. Get out, he said, and looked down, and so I did. Waste of time, he said, while I closed the door. Not long until I was gone. His letters from Brooklyn came back to me at Los Alamos after the censor, everything he said about construction blocked out with long black ink.

Sometime that summer the Army Corps made a baseball field out of desert and nothing, once they were done with the scientific installations. Oppenheimer thought it was good to have us doing something other than work and drink. It was mostly popular with the military men, who played pepper and hit fungoes. But some of the scientists would go watch, and a few number theorists from California made a pretty good infield. Lise liked to sit behind home plate with a skirt on and her legs crossed.

She told me once when I was sitting in her office that she thought I could try to apply myself in ways outside of work, so the next day I went down to the dugout when they were choosing up teams. All anyone wore was T-shirts and jeans then out west, except for the soldiers, of course, who did everything in semi-uniform. One of the sergeants was from Sheepshead Bay and told the number theorists to take me for their outfield. They gave me a glove, and when I ran by, Lise raised her eyebrows and crossed her arms.

I only got one at-bat that day, because they rang an air-raid drill in the second inning. I walked on four pitches, and Lise clapped, and I was looking so much toward her that the PFC playing first base picked me off. I didn't even go back to the dugout, just sat next to her on the bleachers, and she said to me, very sincerely, it could have been worse. I had been worried the whole time in right field about getting a fly ball. I'd never been much good back in Brooklyn. It was a high sky, and that sun was along the first-base line, and I imagined the ball and the sun in my field of vision obscuring each other. I felt sick imagining the ball making two-run-double contact with the ground.

Of course Lise was the love of the whole place. During the dances she told me, when we sat together afterward, that she tried to time each turn with a guy so each one got two and a half minutes. Everyone asked her for dinner, and walks, most of which she declined. She liked being with me, she said, because she knew I was here for the right reasons. What are those? I asked.

Do you miss home? she said. I told her.

What do you think will happen when it ends?

I didn't have an answer.

I'm going to miss the sand of it. She had her shoes off and was drawing circles with her toes.

Look, I said, it's us. I drew another circle to make a Venn diagram.

She put her hands around me then, and I only felt her smile.

She liked to listen to music while she worked, particularly

piano, and I found her a record player in town. Sometimes I brought my drawings into her office too and watched her working, me tracing the air currents things leave when they fall at terminal velocity. There were more and more people running down the halls at that time, and sometimes they came and asked for our pieces of paper. Sometimes you heard people shout in the corridors, and nobody came out and checked if anyone was hurt anymore, because it would just be someone doing something important.

We had been there for a few months, Lise and I, when they got enough uranium to run a test. On the morning of Trinity, I was the last one on top of the tower. We were dropping it from fifteen stories up. One of the chemists had asked an explosives man standing near me at breakfast that morning, wouldn't the tower look conspicuous to everyone after we did the drop? The guy just looked at him.

I was at the top fixing the packaging, making sure the angle was right so it wouldn't hit the scaffolding on the way down. The Gadget had a three-foot radius, and in the tests I ran, it could have a horizontal variance of three inches before the blow. I'd told them to make the drop chute at least eight feet wide, and they gave it ten. It was the middle of a rainstorm, and the lightning was coming down all around me. You could see it hit the desert and the chain-link fences around our compound. Obviously it occurred to me that on top of a metal tower next to the Gadget wasn't the safest place to be with lightning dropping, but someone had to do it. I had heard the theorist squad two days ago asking if everyone was sure this wasn't going to blow holes in the atmosphere. Because then we'd really be cooked. I got off the tower and they drove us ten miles away to a bunker.

Two guys from Washington were there to observe, and they

were standing a few people away from me. Oppenheimer told everyone to squat on their knees. Then he made us turn in the opposite direction of the tower. Ten seconds before it happened he told us to put our palms over our eyes. The Washington guys looked at each other and one said, What'd we come all this way for then? But they did it and then it dropped and we saw our white bones under the skin of our hands.

That night Lise and I climbed out her window onto the roof. One of the German émigrés was playing Tchaikovsky two buildings over. She wanted to dance, and we did, and it was good to be doing something, getting the motion out of our veins. The dust was still coming down at the edge of the horizon, and it was still colored green and purple and pink from the radiation. The thing just blew. I wanted to jump, or pound my fist on the rooftops, or cover Lise with my entire life up to now. Something happened. Something had changed. When Lise pulled off my belt, I almost ripped the top of her blouse. The chipped paint scratched up my back. Later, she asked, Was that your first time? And I lied.

We heard the news about the Gadget going overseas in the morning. There were loudspeakers set up around the compound on top of telephone poles. They played the national anthem and then a sober-voiced man said the tests had worked as well as our wildest dreams. There was champagne at the laboratory benches. Someone was pouring bourbon from imported bottles into beakers, and we toasted.

Lise was with the observation team that was going over to help the crew's training for three weeks. We put a chair under the doorknob in her bathroom and her roommate just knocked and knocked. When she tried to get out, I threw her back against the shower again and again. Her eyes got wide and then wider. We ran to the landing strip, which they'd doubled in size over two weekends.

They dressed the observational team in fatigues, and a lot of us, including Oppenheimer, went to wave the plane good-bye.

During that time we played a lot of pickup baseball on the compound. We were waiting for the OK to get started on the new project, working with hydrogen, 400,000 times more powerful. Everyone was banging on the chalkboards to get going, but Washington said wait. Oppenheimer was traveling back and forth from the East Coast.

The field was yellow with half straw at this heat in August, though the Army Corps people watered the diamond every other week. There was a layer of fine sand over the infield base paths, which made it easy to get grounders. You could just sit back and wait for them to die and swirl in the dust. I liked taking rounds and rounds with the number theorists and some privates, switching off who would hit and then getting in line, seeing who would let the ball through their legs first. It was a game my father would play with other handymen, in the one part of the park that had dry dirt. I had a letter from him, and the un-blacked-out part said, *Double-decker boardwalk canceled, from —— to —— Island. No more restaurants on the top half ——* I didn't read the rest. It didn't feel right in letters. The bat was made of aspen wood from a tree on the compound, and some genius had carved on the power spot, *Los Alamos, Home of Explosions*. We spent long afternoons there, lying in the dusty outfield, looking at the sun. It was a pulsing, living thing that summer, its image burned into our retinas while we waited.

When Lise came back I went to meet the plane, and I asked her if she wanted to go to the cantina for a drink. The particle physicist from the office next to hers was holding a banner, and they were pumping music through the loudspeakers. I tried to press the khaki of her shirt against my chest. But she pushed me off and went to her room. When she came out she was in civilian clothes and she wanted to get dinner. In town we were stopped at a green light waiting for jeeps to go by, and she told me she wasn't going to stay.

We argued. We sat against somebody else's fence and never made it to dinner. I said that technically the military police could get involved. She said that the second bomb had shattered the trees rather than blowing them over. I told her she had an obligation to her country and her brother, a Marine in the Fifth. She said there were shadows of spiral staircases on walls where the staircases were gone. That the *Enola Gay* flew through a late moon in the east. That there were eight ships in Hiroshima Harbor. That she hadn't slept since somewhere over the Pacific. I stopped her and touched her hand and asked if she remembered the night of Trinity, and she sneered, I hardly remember. Really? I said. Grow up, she said, and I slammed my hand through the fence. She got up and walked away slowly while some mother came out and started to squawk.

It took a week for her clearance to be revoked, and for all the papers to come in for her statements to be signed. She ate dinner with me once, but she wouldn't dance afterward. She stayed inside with a handful of other scientists who were leaving while we toasted, in the middle of the street, next to the pagoda the Army Corps had just finished installing. We went for walks and sat on the bench in the dugout when the baseball field was empty, and for a while she was almost like always. But then that Friday she wouldn't say a word, and she didn't want me to touch her shoulders. I gave it up. You have to leave some behind.

Two days later she was gone and we got the go-ahead to get the H-bomb up and running. The war was over but the Russians were working on their own Gadget, and it was only a matter of time before this one mattered. Everyone was ecstatic. We worked twelve-hour days, talked only about fusion. I dropped metal from the rooftops to measure the lateral drift. She left and I hated that she had, with all this going on. It started again, the nights in the cantina, the days in underground labs. The military men played baseball, but we had a war on here. Sometimes I caught myself panting in the middle of drafting, and I'd have to take a beaker of bourbon before starting again. I knew guys who had to be hospitalized for refusing to sleep. There was talk of changing our sleep schedules to make a twenty-six-hour day. Day and night became interchangeable. Lise wrote a letter, saying she was somewhere in Arizona and trying to live. I threw it out. I wanted to see it again, the cloud coming over the desert. So loud that the deaf heard something outrageous and the blind asked if this was white. I went into her office, pored over her papers, sat in the plush chair behind her desk. I began to think that she took the answer with her. She knew how it could be done. There was a secret and it was lost to me. She was gone and we were waiting for inspiration to strike.

FOR YOU

Because she is not with you, you get off the train, late one night, and you go to the bar. The bar is on Bergen and off Smith Street. You walk past it every day, on your way to the F train. On the way home at night you walk past it again, with the hordes of other people, all in their black jackets and suits, sometimes blue, for the women. You've done that walk with her, walked by the bar, though she refuses to wear blue. Sorry, Eamon, she'd say. You almost forgot that. Tonight you go in. It is a late night. The white bartender, as you come through the door, gives you the look that he gives to desperate people. We just had last call, he says. Can I get a drink? you say. I'm sorry, says the bartender. Just one, you say, as you slide into an empty stool at the bar, facing the newly exposed red brick. The bartender looks over his shoulder, and then he looks at the door, where a man has just entered, maybe Hispanic, a man who at first looks worn and weather-beaten and then you realize it's just the coat he has on, and the style with which he holds his shoulders. Other than that he is a young man, your age, maybe, no more. The bartender leans close to you and says, Just one. I don't want to create a rush. That's fine, you tell him, as the man settles into the seat next to yours. I'll have the pale ale, you tell him, and you do.

You sip the pale ale like you've never had a drink before, as if it were a religious ceremony. You look at the exposed brick walls. You still have your hood on, and your collar turned up, on the black coat you are wearing.

The bartender comes up to the man sitting next to you and his friends. *Otro?* he asks. *Nada más,* says the man, and the bartender says, *No te preocupas.* You snort, to show you've understood it, and because you have, the man sitting next to you says, You speak Spanish?

And you say, *Solo un poco.*

And he says, That's good, that's good.

And you say, *De dónde son ustedes?*

And he answers once again in English. From Arizona, he says. Pointing at the young man next to him, he says, Miami. And then the attractive woman at the end of the bar. Guatemala. She nods.

And you? the Arizona man says, in the English version of the *y tu* that you would have understood.

I'm from here, you say—from Brooklyn. Marine Park. Down that way. You point in a vague southerly direction.

Arizona looks surprised.

I've never met anyone who's actually from here before.

You laugh and consider bringing up the E. B. White line that's on the subway posters, but instead you just say, That's the way it is.

It's different from here, down there, you say. He nods. But not so different. There are more things to do in this part. He nods again.

Many things to do here, he says. Many restaurants.

Lots of restaurants, you say. Lots of exposed brick, you add, pointing at the walls. They used to be covered with plaster, you say, as if you know. The woman from Guatemala leans over and says, Plaster? And suddenly you are very tired. Yes, you say, and leave it at that.

You drink more of your pale ale and the two men and woman

go back to speaking to each other in low tones in Spanish. The bartender walks out from behind the bar, which is still crowded, and goes out the door. You decide not to look at your cell phone. When the bartender comes back into his bar, he walks by the man from Arizona, and slips a wad of napkins into his coat pocket, his coat still on. There is the smell, suddenly, that overcomes you, like wet earth, like lying on the grass somewhere with trees. The man from Arizona looks at you. You look at him.

It's OK, you say. You're among friends.

Can you smell it? he asks.

Sure, you say.

You need a ziplock bag, his companion says. Do you have a ziplock bag? he asks you.

I don't, you say. But it's fine. I can only smell it because I'm so close, you add. He closes his jacket more and grins at you. David, he says, and extends his hand. You shake it. You tell him your name. We're waiters, he says. But we have money. We live in Carroll Gardens. Me and Andreo. Isabella is in Brooklyn Heights. But Isabella has already stopped paying attention to you and her fellow workers, and is busy looking at her cell phone.

What restaurant? you say. Is it one I might have been to?

Maybe, they say, and they name a restaurant on Smith Street that you have never been to. You never eat in restaurants alone.

I know it, you say. A nice place. A good place.

They nod noncommittally. Yes, David says, but not like Arizona. Andreo agrees.

What do you mean? you say.

No tipping like Arizona, he says. In Arizona they tip 40 percent.

Forty percent, you say, too loud, as if you might have been outraged.

Yes, David says. It is common.

And how about here? you ask.

David thinks for a minute, swilling the wine that is left in his glass. Ten, fifteen. Sometimes twenty, he says. Sometimes five. Sometimes point oh-oh-oh-oh-oh-one percent.

Jesus, you say. So do you know, like, when a table sits down, how much they'll tip you?

David nods, but he looks uncomfortable. He is holding his glass just a little above the bar, resting it on his fist. How do you know? you say. Is it racial?

David says yes, when you force him to. Who's worst? you say, triumphant. David looks over his shoulder. Black people, he says. Not all of them, he adds, quickly. There are rules and exceptions.

Of course, you say. How about white people? David shrugs. They're OK. Sometimes they feel bad for us. And Latinos? you ask. Oh, the best, David says. Andreo agrees.

You all look at the wall together, as the bar empties out around you. Isabella, who works in the kitchen, leaves, because she is meeting a man whom the other two don't know, who comes to pick her up in a car. You wonder who owns a car in this neighborhood. You don't. You thought about getting one, the two of you, when she was there, sharing the registration, putting your two names on it. You had talked about the places you could drive. Skiing upstate. You don't know how to ski, she said. A weekend in New Jersey. The Catskills. I'll believe it when it happens, she said. You rarely plan for anything. It seems nice, you like it best, when things carry you along their way. You were never one for omens. Recently you were walking by a billboard near the BQE, and when you looked up, a young man that you knew from elementary school was staring down at you, a smiling senior at St. Francis College. It was an old poster. Some of the center was showing through, so you could see an ad for Kars4Kids. You know it is that ad, because you've seen it many times before. You never get farther than the BQE, but some days, walking by there, hearing the trucks scream by, you think about hitchhiking across the country to see her. It could happen. It could be done.

The smell from David's pocket is still pungent, and it makes you feel vigorous and safe. What do you do? David asks.

You dismiss this with a wave of your hand. This and that, you say. But then you tell them. They nod noncommittally. Their disinterest vaguely alarms you. It reminds you that you are in a bar sitting next to two people who you've never met before. You wonder how long this can go on for. Desperate now, with the pale ale down to its last fingers, and the bartender swabbing the counter with a greasy, heavy rag, you turn to David and Andreo and you say, What are your hopes and dreams?

And they take this question at face value. They nurture it, turn it over in their heads. They mull it like the wine that they are drinking, that they are finishing. Both have double shifts in the morning, starting at nine a.m.

David answers first, and says, I want to work in nonprofits. This you dismiss with your own disinterest, and you say to Andreo, What about you?

Andreo works his hands out of the folds of his coat, and he puts them both in the air, and he says, I want to use these, and he waves them.

What do you mean? you ask him.

I want to be a writer, he says. I want to write news.

And you swell up with a joy that doesn't make sense at the time, as he tells you about enrolling in classes in the CUNY journalism school. Do you know CUNY? he asks. Of course you know

CUNY—who doesn't? You want to take his name, his number, watch for his byline in the morning paper, or on Internet updates: *Reporting contributed by Andreo—,* from Brooklyn, Washington, Miami, Kandahar. It will happen, you tell him, you lie to him. It will. And he smiles, and puts his hands back in his pockets, and knows that things will change.

You walk outside and David and Andreo shake hands with you, and they don't offer to share the sweet smell in David's pocket, but they confirm that they do go to this bar often, and you think that maybe you might frequent it, on the way home from work, from your office in the city, riding on the black backs of suits and jackets. Maybe you might stop, have a drink, find Andreo, ask him about his work, before going home to the empty apartment, where the only view is billboards.

You walk home. The lights on Pacific Street are all off. All the streets here are named for oceans, as if the ocean might reclaim them, any day. Inside your apartment, you take off the wet shoes on your feet, the wet socks. You take off your black jacket, your sweatshirt with a hood. You look at the pictures on your walls and find that the drink doesn't help anymore, and you pick up the phone and you make a call across the country.

You hold your breath until she picks up. You haven't talked in a while. Hello? she says. Hello? Eamon, she says, and that lets you speak.

Hello, you say. I missed you. I missed you tonight. She sighs into the speaker, and says that she missed you too. The phone connection isn't enough for you, and you ask her if she has her computer nearby, and you connect to the Internet, and through the magic of machines and cameras she is in front of you, in pajamas, her hair tied on top of her head.

You can't say anything. You don't. You don't want to talk about anything at all anymore. You don't tell her about David or Andreo or the sweet smell or the car that took Isabella away. That is all over now, like another lifetime, and the waiters fade to nothing in your head.

Are you OK? she asks you, and you shake your head, one way and then the other. You're making me upset, she tells you. And because you don't know what else to do, and you don't want to make her upset, you reach a hand out toward the computer screen, even though you know it can't do anything. You reach a hand to where her hand is on her computer screen, as if to hold it. You hold nothing but the hot section of the screen itself, the energy of keeping your pictures alive pumping up out of it, like a stove. You watch her, your hands almost touching, the swirls in her palm visible on the high-definition screen, and it is as close as you can come, or as much as she can give you, for you.

HAIRCUT

n the afternoon, Andrew went to Marine Park to get a haircut. He'd been at an interview in the morning, for a job that would make him not rich but comfortable, more comfortable than now—with the possibility of riches, of an extra house in the Hamptons, if you followed the curve of the borough out into the Atlantic. At the interview, one partner at the firm had asked if he could tell a little about himself, his fingers hanging from the résumé like bangs, the paper resting on the crook of his arm. Well, Andrew said, I grew up in Brooklyn. Marine Park, he said. The partners nodded. I've been working in the city mostly since college. The résumé partner stopped him. That's funny, he said. How so? Andrew asked. Only a true Brooklynite would say going into the city. The partners grinned together, as if their grins connected into one grin. It's true, Andrew said.

The barber's was nearly empty this late in the afternoon. Andrew had come after work, had driven down Ocean Parkway, past the Q train at Kings Highway, Quentin Road for the last few blocks. He hadn't told anyone he'd be coming. At the barber's, Javi, who had been cutting his hair since he was a child, was looking at the sports cycle on the television bolted into the wall above his chair. He was scrolling through his phone. Hey, Andrew said. My friend, said Javi. Have a seat. I have no one. Andrew sat and Javi wrapped the light black tarpaulin of a smock around him. Underneath Andrew felt cool and dry, while Javi went to work, without talking, on his head.

Before Andrew got contacts, he had relished the surprise that came after taking off his glasses at the beginning and staring blankly, unseeingly, at the mirror while Javi worked. The clip of Javi's scissors vibrated from one ear to another—ever since Andrew had decided that he didn't want just a buzz cut, that he was looking for something more sophisticated. Buzz cuts had been summer haircuts, for when he and his friends were playing the St. Thomas Aquinas basketball camp near Flatbush, run by Chris Mullen, the archetype of the neighborhood, who'd gotten out in a big way. He'd played for Xaverian, starred there, was a white kid in an era when there were few. He played in a white way, as far as Andrew could remember, even when he was teaching the clinics—jump shots, dribbling drills. Nothing much like inspiration. What Andrew had liked better were the nuns peering over the hedges at the outdoor basketball hoops they set up for those months. While the boys ran bare-chested up and down the asphalt, shouting for the ball, skinning knees, the nuns sat in plastic chairs propped against the thin fences, watching, or continuing their circumnavigations around the garden. The garden looked cool and inviting to Andrew, surrounded by trees, without the heat echo of the basketball courts.

When he was older, after college, before the time when he returned home to the city, he lived near a lake in New England where he thought about that sort of thing. He had found a job as an executive assistant in the office of an insurance company, next to the lake. In the afternoons, after work, during which he sat mindlessly in the office shuttling emails from one person to another, looking out the window; after that, he'd go to the basketball court, get in as many five-on-fives as he could. The competition wasn't as good as New York, but it was something. His jump shot, which had never been his strong suit, was back with a vengeance during that time. He found that he could roll off picks, create just the smallest of spaces between him and the defender, make the shot. Midrange Mac is here, some of the regulars said when he showed up in his Camry. Keep him out past the three-point line.

But in the mornings, to wake up, to get the resolve he needed before the office back-and-forth started, he went swimming. The office loomed in front of him. It was the type of experience that would become so entrenched later in life that it would be hard to look back at this moment and think of a time when offices were new. They were life now; then they were soul-sucking. Those mornings, he'd drive to a parking spot in the woods, shedding his khakis and blazer on the backseat, and he'd walk down to the empty lake, the tight green around it and the cool air coming off the water. He walked into the water, never ran, swam out as far toward the far-side trees as he could, turned over, looked up. When he was ready he swam back.

At the barber's Javi was talking to him. It wasn't usual, that Javi talked to him. There had been a time once when he wanted a conversation with his barber, after having read old stories about barbers singing in your ear, giving all the political conversation. But not after looking at a computer screen all day, reading news reports and industry updates, his only break from the machine when he walked to the bathroom, which his company docked half an hour of pay for each day. They assumed half an hour each day was what people usually spent. They wanted employees to be in their seats, emailing with the companies they represented. After hours of that, Andrew looked forward to the period of useful silence, of animated quiet, that the trip to the barber's provided. How there was no sound, and he could hibernate in his own head, because someone else was already working.

Javi was asking about work. How it was, whether he liked it. Whether he'd had time to go to a Mets game this season.

Work's fine, Andrew said. We just got the crop of summer interns in, so it's making life a little easier for the junior consultants.

That's good, Javi said, encouraging.

And it's always nice to see some young people, especially of the female persuasion, Andrew said. He grinned and looked up at Javi to grin with him. But perhaps he hadn't heard. Andrew looked back in the mirror and remembered that Javi had a daughter. He wasn't sure if that kind of thing mattered.

Your father has not been in in a while, Javi announced.

Huh, Andrew said. He didn't know why this would be. He said so. Think he needs a haircut? Andrew said.

Oh yes, said Javi, everybody needs haircuts. Especially in the summer. It keeps the cool in the head. Very important. You can keep cool heads.

Andrew shifted in his chair. He watched the sculpting of his head that was taking place in the mirror. Don't people usually have cool heads around here? Andrew asked. That's sort of what Marine Park is, no? A bunch of cool heads?

Javi cut a difficult part around the ear and nodded slowly. Yes, he said, but sometimes no. He went on to elaborate how the other day, while he'd been on his way to work, walking down Quentin Road, he saw a crowd surrounding a man lying on the sidewalk, and when he got closer he realized that a woman was screaming next to him, or trying to scream. She was screaming in a way by which you could tell she'd been screaming for a long time. Javi asked if someone should do something, and the man next to him, in a firehouse T-shirt, said that the trucks were already on their way. Another man in a firehouse T-shirt was kneeling with the man on the ground, trying to hold his arms away from his head, which was bleeding. The fireman held the hands down with one of his own, pulled off his T-shirt, wrapped it around the back of the man's bleeding head, to act as a cushion at least, even if he couldn't stop the blood. The bleeding man's hands continued reaching for the blood spot on his head. Javi shook his head, asked the obligatory question. Someone next to him said, A hammer. He got into a shouting match, and the attacker pulled a hammer out of his backpack. The man stood his ground, because he couldn't believe that anything would happen. Then the hammer man stepped forward and started swinging. The bleeding man fell. Finally something snapped in the hammer man, and he stopped swinging, and ran away.

Andrew had turned to look at Javi while he told the story, the scissors fallen to Javi's side. Did the man who told you all this see it happen? Andrew asked. Javi shrugged. Sure, I think so. Andrew pressed, He saw it with his own eyes? Someone with a hammer? Javi shook his head again. People are people, he said. I heard what I heard. They all had long hair, he added. Not good in the summer.

Andrew walked out of the barber shop, past the funeral parlor and the Park Bench Cafe. From behind him, he heard a voice, and he turned around.

Hey, Javi was saying, looking up and struggling with his key in the barbershop door. Can you give me a lift?

Andrew nodded and extended his hand toward where his car

was parked, across the street. It was the same Camry. If he got the new job he'd buy a new car. The Camry was a hand-me-down, the type of thing that was good for a late twentysomething. Andrew looked at the car as he opened it. It wasn't the type of thing you'd put a wife in. Or a child.

Kings Highway, asked Andrew, is that where you're going? He fiddled with his seat belt.

Well, said Javi. He was wiping stray pieces of hair off his hands, onto the floor in the passenger seat. Andrew wondered if it was his hair.

Could we make a stop? Javi asked. It's a little embarrassing.

Andrew drove and Javi directed. Up to the light on Quentin. A left on Marine Parkway, the wide street that looked like Paris. Andrew had heard once that real estate agents were telling gentrifiers that that was the beauty of the neighborhood: the wide Parisian streets. Andrew wondered whether middle class neighborhoods could be gentrified. He didn't expect to see many coffee shops. Though even Ditmas Park was getting crowded. Left on Avenue U, Javi said.

Andrew pulled into the Avenue U parking lot, which was nearly empty of cars. One SUV had its trunk open, playing Jamaican dance hall music. There was a cricket game happening at that side of the park, though it seemed to Andrew like it was miles away. The SUV was full of men and women watching the game, people lounging on the side. In the corner, where during the winter a company comes to sell Christmas trees, there was a small white car, which at first glance you would think was a woman's car. Andrew wasn't sure why—the color and the careful polish? Here, Javi said. When he got out, the door of the white car opened, and then Andrew grinned, because it was Ed Monahan.

Andrew watched the two of them converse from his car. Ed

didn't get out of the driver's seat. Andrew remembered Ed when they were kids playing basketball in the park. Andrew had been taller, stronger, played center all the way through, but Ed was the real prodigy, had a basketball scholarship to Molloy High School, even though he was one of the shortest guys on Good Shepherd. Andrew had never seen, before or since, on the street courts of the cities he'd lived in, a ball handler as good, one who was as tenacious getting rebounds and looking for the upcourt pass. Ed was the type of kid who, when he was getting refused entry to street games even if it was his rightful next, would take a ball from where it was resting against the chain-link fence and begin spidering, faster and faster, just to show he could. Sometimes the games stopped. More often someone just yelled, Let Whitey in. Ed would stop the wild motions then, hold the ball breathing heavy against his side, flushed with victory, convinced that he was, as everyone told him, good enough. If Andrew remembered right he'd walked on to St. Joseph's for college—they were looking for a backup point guard. But the starter, a real beautiful kid from the South Bronx, never gave him a chance, and Ed only played the one year. When he came back he didn't have it in him to take the fireman test, wait on that line. Someone had told Andrew he was working sanitation.

As Javi walked back Andrew stuck his head out the window. Hey, Ed, he called. Hey. Ed Monahan looked up from where he was counting bills, startled. It's Andrew. Andrew Dempsey, Andrew said. Ed squinted, his dirty ponytail shaking, like he wasn't sure if Andrew was supposed to be an undercover cop or something— Marine Park had those too. Government employees popping up like McCain signs. How ya doing? Andrew asked, and Ed nodded. You know, fine, fine, all is good. Still playing ball? Andrew asked. Ed peered at him like he was crazy, and then pressed the button to pull his window up.

Javi opened the passenger-side door, putting the ziplock bag in his jeans pocket. Sorry, my friend, he said. Just quick, no problem. Andrew grinned at him. Javi smiled back. Do you want? he asked. Andrew considered. He hadn't smoked since college, when there were weeks he remembered being high even on the basketball court. Playing pickup, only being able to play one game, because of the kick to the lungs, feeling glorious. But he was expecting to get the new consulting job. It was the type of thing that came with a drug test. They'd probably still be interviewing for the position, and he needed to give his two weeks' notice. Come on, Javi said. I have one of these, he said, and pulled a one-hitter from his pocket, shaped like a cigarette, where the red glow of the ember could hang on the nether end.

There came a time when they were driving again, Andrew driving. He was upset to find that he didn't feel much of anything, though he was relaxed. He couldn't remember a time he was as relaxed as he was now. He hadn't been back to Marine Park in a month, the last time he'd seen his parents. When will you have a girlfriend, Drew? his mother asked. Isn't it time for that yet? You're at work too much. His father sat at the kitchen counter, his undershirt tucked into his pants, reading the *Daily News*. Why don't you consult for this government? he said. They're shit out of luck. Might as well waste money another way. Isn't it? his mother asked, still on the girlfriend.

A right here, Javi was saying. They were driving along the water, where the nature center was, a plot of open land. Andrew opened the window to let it out. Straight now, Javi said. They were on Gerritsen Avenue, going down.

Andrew found himself saying it as he was saying it. What do you talk to my father about, Javi, when you cut his hair? Javi looked at him strangely. Talk? he asked. We don't talk. I cut. He sits. What talking? Andrew nodded sagely. It's true, Andrew said.

They were next to the old public library. It was the end of the road. If you went farther, you hit the water. To the right there were stores and houses, and the library. And to the left there was a basketball court. I need to get one thing here, Javi said. For going home. He left and walked to the right. Andrew sat and watched the road in front of him. Then he got out of the car.

It was a basketball court that he hadn't remembered ever being there before. Once he'd prided himself on knowing all the basketball courts in the neighborhood. They all had their character, like different positions. The Marine Park main courts, showcase courts—when the *Times* wrote a piece about basketball in the city, they mentioned it. The old men putting up tents between the courts and playing dominos. Read: black, but the newspaper didn't say it. The newspaper didn't mention Orthodox Jewish point guards reaching for their yarmulkes; the black men, polite, pausing the game if the yarmulkes fell off. You had to kiss them first, even Andrew knew that. It was the only thing a game stopped for. After, everyone went off in their own cars, to their own neighborhoods.

This basketball court, it didn't have anything like that, just a couple kids, a guy and his girlfriend, playing Horse on the far court closer to the water. Some other kids hanging on the benches, drinking something. Not a court near the water like Manhattan, where the water was a character in itself—not like a vacation home. The water was an accident here. It was rough grass and overgrown baseball fields until Gerritsen Creek, Dead Horse Bay.

Andrew watched the guy and girlfriend taking turns shooting, his fingers in the chain-link fence. He had never been the type of kid who dribbled a basketball wherever he went; it was too showy. He took one with him, held against his side, to the park on off times, to practice his shot. There was a certain symmetry to it, the shot and the rebound, alone, the plodding along. The way you could continue to do the same thing over and over again, the only difference being the angle, the force of the shot off your fingers.

Behind him, he heard a car drive up and slow. Andrew turned. It was a white car, clean and overwaxed. Andrew squinted at the window and he thought it was Ed Monahan's car, Ed's squirrel face behind the half-tinted glass. The car stopped. It seemed like there was a face turned to watch, scowling. Then the car started again, and fled, and Andrew turned around.

He heard the last bounce of the ball. The girlfriend stood with the ball against her stomach, the boyfriend in front of her. A girl from the crowd of drinkers was yelling at them.

Want to see ghetto? the girl was saying. Want to see ghetto? I'll show you ghetto. And she stomped, in the way of earth-shattering steps, to where the girlfriend was standing. She grabbed her hair, and started to pull her down.

Things got complicated then. Andrew would read about it in the *Gazette* some days later, but he could never tell if it was right in its entirety. The boyfriend pushed the hair-puller away; another boy came up to him with a box cutter. Andrew didn't see a slash, more just two forward motions, and the boy moaned. The girlfriend was on the ground and someone was stomping on her chest. People were running by Andrew from the shops across the street, onto the court like a full-court press, trying to break the thing up, but Andrew couldn't move. The baseline, painted white, was streaked with blood. A mob of people was on the court. And Andrew, Andrew walked slowly away, back to his car. Slowly he crossed the street and left the basketball court behind him.

Some moments later, a hand knocked on the passenger-side window. Javi was standing there, smiling, holding a bouquet of flowers. Andrew leaned over to open the door. For the daughter, Javi said.

Andrew drove slowly, as if he could no longer afford speed. He didn't think Javi had seen anything. He didn't think he would have to explain—the girl stomping forward, extending her arms. They did not speak in the car, with the sun starting to go down, the arch-necked streetlights coming on. Javi kept twirling the top of his hair. He hummed softly, even though the radio was on.

Javi had told Andrew once about where he came from, a Mexican valley somewhere. His family, father and sons, mother and daughters, all were haircutters. They had been to school for it. Only Javi had come to America. It was colder here, Javi said, but often cold there in the winter. Being near the water made it temperate. In the winter, some months, Javi took up and left, went with his daughter back to Mexico, closed the shop. Andrew remembered looking at the sign, the lights off.

At the train they shook hands, hard clasps, fingers tight. OK, my friend, Javi said. All finished. He took his bouquet and left. Andrew watched as he put the flowers in his teeth to use the MetroCard, to swipe himself through.

Andrew began to drive, aimlessly. He needed to go back to his apartment in the city, park the car in the parking garage below the building, which he paid good money for. He had to be at work at eight thirty, something that didn't seem likely to change, at the new job if he got it or anytime in the future. He imagined waking up to get to work at eight thirty for an unimaginable stretch ahead, the long days passing like opposite-lane cars.

Where could he go? He could go to the house where he grew up, watch the light die with his parents. He could park on their block, walk in, ring the bell, and watch their surprised faces. Talk to them about the future. He did not. He went off R to Fillmore, to the edge of the park, the Marine Park basketball courts, spread out on the corner of the green.

Just before he got to the chain-link, someone yelled from behind him. Hey, the voice said. Andrew turned. It was Ed Monahan. Hey, Ed said again. What's the idea? You following me around or something? Up this close Ed looked more haggard than he used to. He looked smaller than Andrew remembered, though his arms were taut. What're you doing back here anyway? I heard you were a city man now. Ed was just below Andrew's face. His forearms, hairy and muscular, twitched.

Listen Ed, Andrew started, but he couldn't finish it. He wanted nothing more than a game of basketball. A good one-on-one game, the feel of a body hitting another body, bouncing off, hitting again. Something he hadn't felt in a while.

Listen, he said vaguely.

You listen, said Ed. Get back in your car, pussy, and get away.

So Andrew hit him. He couldn't remember the last time he'd thrown a punch. His hand, as it connected with the bones in Ed's face, broke—or that's what it felt like. The knuckles moved up, higher than his fingers, though that didn't make physical sense. Ed staggered back, and then he was on him.

Andrew found himself on the pavement, his face getting hit from side to side. He had that anxious feeling of first blood, the adrenaline jumping through the veins to tell the body, all is fine. A few minutes later it wouldn't feel that way anymore, and it would just be pain, until someone pulled Ed away, with flashing lights. On the pavement, Andrew imagined many things. He imagined that it was a basketball fight he'd gotten into, a righteous one; that someone had called a hard foul and he was upholding the call, and then the perpetrator attacked. He imagined that his face, black and blue and purple the next morning probably, would look like a bouquet of flowers, cherry red with dried blood and green the stems for all the infected parts. And he imagined that Ed Monahan, on top of him until he was pulled off, was having a harder time than he might have, because he had no grip on Andrew's head, his newly cut hair not long enough to hold on to. Andrew felt thankful for his haircut, for the cool breeze he felt passing by his neck.

ED MONAHAN'S GAME

Way down south and east and close to the water, where Avenue U runs parallel to the salt marsh, and the sounds of the trucks heading toward the Belt Parkway keep sane people up at night, in a house that used to belong to his parents lives Ed Monahan. Some nights Ed stays up shivering, thinking of all the ills that befall this country. Sometimes while he watches the news he thinks of ways things could be better. He owns a gun, the same one his daddy did, his daddy who was a police detective, and worked as a court officer once he retired. One day in the court Ed Monahan's father worked in, a man made it around the metal detectors that the technicians were just installing, back before they were mandatory, and in the middle of the grand jury proceedings the man, who had been brought in to be a witness, stood up and fired three shots at the defendant on the stand. Two missed. Ed Monahan's father, who had been seated at the front with his arms crossed, keeping his eye on the defendant, who in his opinion looked "shifty," took one step forward and raised his gun. With one bullet, he downed the shooter. It was a true shot, but the shooter survived, and went on trial and got fifteen years prison. It was the first time Ed Monahan's father had fired his gun. Niggers, he said.

In the morning, Ed Monahan, who had never successfully held

down a full-time job, gathered his belongings and his merchandise and packed them onto his bicycle, in wide burlap motorcycle packs he'd bought from the army surplus store on Atlantic Avenue. He put in all the string shaving cream, fire snaps, boxes of hard candy that wouldn't melt, and toy BB guns that made clicks when you pressed the trigger down rapidly. He had a ponytail that he washed every morning. He had a girlfriend who some nights slept over, who would take her clothes off and lie naked beside him, while he struggled to get himself prepared—though this morning she was not. He had black T-shirts that he wore every day with his jeans. When he had his T-shirt on, over the wifebeater, gray from hand-washing and age, that he wore even in the summer, he wheeled his packed bicycle out of the house and toward the open street by Avenue U. Summers, he had a job to do. He was saving up to buy a car. He got up early. He felt good about himself. He got on his bike and rode the couple of blocks toward the playground in Marine Park.

Basketball was the only thing he'd ever enjoyed. Nobody else really understood it, or understood what it meant to him. His father hadn't—had only wanted him to get taller and stronger and faster, fast enough to beat the black kids in CYO ball, when Ed Monahan played for Good Shepherd. For a while, he was—tall and strong and fast enough. But some things don't stay like that forever, and his growth spurt ended at fifteen. He held on for a couple years, even walking onto a team in college. But a kid from the projects got the point guard job instead of him, and he quit after the first year. My kid doesn't ride pine, Ed Monahan's father said proudly. Now Ed only watched the Knicks at the Mariners Inn, every once in a while. He hated, with an intensity, the people who were diehard fans and wouldn't miss a game.

This was the Mariners Inn that Ed Monahan biked slowly by, where the firemen, retired or on disability, stood outside to have a smoke. Morning, Ed, one of them said, as Ed passed. Ed nodded back, and his thin ponytail bounced up and down. Almost out of earshot, the retired fireman said, Fag, and put out his cigarette and went inside. Ed Monahan kept biking.

At the playground, Ed made an exploratory circle on his bicycle. It was the type of day where everybody was around the sprinkler in the middle, kids and adults. Some of the adults were parents—firemen or cops on their off hours, office workers on vacation. There were grandmothers and grandfathers, still trim in polo shirts tucked into their shorts. They looked like they could outrun Ed, still. Ed hadn't kept his speed up, though he was still trim. He blamed it on the cigarettes. Because Ed hadn't played football as a kid, even though he was an absolute wizard at basketball, the rest of the neighborhood youth disowned him. His nickname was Pussy Ed, all the way up to seventh grade. Even when he led Good Shepherd to the St. Francis de Sale's Christmas Tournament title—but some things can't be overcome.

When he guided his weighed-down bike into the confines of the playground, the grandparents edged a little closer to their grandkids. The parents, some of whom knew Ed, left it alone. Ed pulled in a deep breath, and while doing so he felt that the whole park was holding its breath around him. He yelled: Crackers! Candy! String cream! Under a dollar! The parents looked down at their feet. The children, their heads turning away from the water, came running.

In Ed's business you make your money in dimes and quarters; there's nothing wrong with that. He had blisters on his fingers from the coin roll-ups he was constantly using, to put the money together to bring to the bank. He didn't spend much—he had the house from his daddy. In the winter he worked as an ice guard at the Aviator rink. The coins added up. While the children walked or jogged to him, he heard their coins' metallic bounce in his mind's ear.

How much for Gobstoppers? a chubby little shit in a red bathing suit asked.

Two dollars, said Ed. He'd bought them in quantity, each pack for twenty-five cents.

The chubby kid unrolled two sweaty dollar bills from his hot palms, leaving one unknown bill in his grasp. Here, he said. Gimme.

Is that how you ask for it? said Ed. The kid didn't answer. Ed didn't have anything better to say. Whatever, he said.

The children, in a screen around Ed and his bike, forced their smudged coins and bills on him, some crisp twenties from their parents, to whom he had to return a handful of ones and quarters. The playground, centered before Ed's arrival around the old sprinkler, exploded to the four corners with the sounds of fake gun pops and the rainbow colors of string cream.

One small girl came up to Ed and asked if he was selling jump ropes. Some days he did—cheap plastic ones for which he made a five-dollar profit. Sorry, he told the girl, his ponytail wagging. How about a plastic shooter? He picked out a pink one in its shrink-wrapping from his bag.

My *mother*, the girl said, eye-pointing to a dumpy little woman reading a magazine on a bench, doesn't approve of guns.

Ed looked the woman up and down, on the bench. She was wearing Crocs. He'd heard about those on TV, from commercials during Knicks games at the Mariners. He leaned down close to the little girl, who herself leaned closer to hear what he said. That's some cunt shit, he said. What does that mean? the little girl asked. He had nothing to say.

When one of his saddlebags was noticeably lighter, Ed straddled his bike, pedaled through the playground entrance, passing the woman with the magazine and the fat kid in red shorts, and coasted toward the 0.84-mile oval that was the crown jewel of Marine Park. Coming around the bend, he passed the basketball courts he'd grown up on as a kid, when he was the unlikely underdog, white but good. Filled with black kids still, none of whom could shoot. Ed had to admit, even from a quick glance, and he knew it would continue as he pedaled past them: the kids could play. More athletic than he'd ever been. He heard one of the rims shudder as someone tried to dunk.

In the Avenue U parking lot there were three cars waiting for him. They were pulled up against the green, so that they could have been watching the cricket games. Windows closed, air-conditioning on. When Ed reached the middle of the lot he thought in his head about shouting, Peanuts! Crackerjacks! But it would be unwise— he'd always been lucky about police. Instead, he kickstood his bike up on the edge of the cement, pretended to fix a flat. A husky Irish man got out of a car to talk to him.

Holding? he asked Ed in an undertone.

What I always do, said Ed. But step inside my office.

I don't want much, the man said, fingering the sweat stains on his shirt.

Just take it out of the pack, Ed said. I'm working on a damn tire over here.

The man unzipped the pack, and took out a small ziplock bag. In its place, he left a number of bills. Ed didn't count them, because he didn't have to. That's fine, Ed said. Fine day we having today.

The man, once he had his ziplock bag, didn't look at Ed, as if he had something communicable. He started walking away. Then he turned around.

You be here Wednesday? he said.

Ed sighed. Sure, he said, why not. The man nodded and went back to his car.

Ed Monahan watched the car pull away, skid around the parking lot entrance, shoot down Avenue U. There were some slum spots as you moved away from Marine Park. Who knew where the guy was headed. Ed only sold the soft stuff. He hummed to himself as he fiddled with the tire on his bike—he took faking it to an art form. From behind him, he heard another car door slam. Two more ziplock bags, and he sent them away like children.

There was a tap on his shoulder, and Ed turned around. Hi, honey, his girlfriend Margie said.

Ed looked her over. She was tall in the way that women are and you don't realize it, or, rather, short but because they're women you think they're tall. She was wearing a Guns N' Roses T-shirt, like she usually did. She was skinny. If Ed worried about things he would worry about this, but he didn't. Instead, he pulled her toward him and put her hand on his crotch. Been waiting for you, Ed said.

Margie extracted her hand from where he had placed it, and instead put it on his hip and into his side pocket. She fingered the slightly damp clump of bills he had mushed there. Seems like it, she said, and withdrew some of the clump, and looked at it.

Keep away from that, Ed Monahan said. I worked for that. Whatever, Margie said.

Ed locked his bike up against a telephone pole, and then he and Margie walked across the street to the salt marsh nature center. The cottontails were high this early in summer, the wind off the bay blowing them back and forth. There was a gravel path that had been cut by the Army Corps of Engineers a few years ago, which made it more respectable. Used to be just about anything was growing in and around the waters. Ed took Margie here for walks in the salt marsh often, because he didn't like to pay for the movies.

I went into the city today, Margie was saying. Went shopping.

Yeah? Ed said.

Took an hour and a half to get in, because the Q train was slow.

It happens, Ed said. That's why I don't go. What's the point?

I was thinking maybe the two of us could go in for dinner one night, though, Margie said. Ed pretended that he was fascinated with the view of the Marine Parkway Bridge. Ed? Margie said.

Sure, he said. Maybe. For New Year's or something. I think we could handle that. They arrived at the only tree in the salt marsh. Here, he said. And he sat down.

Margie stayed standing above him.

What? she said.

Come on, Marge, don't make me have to beg, Ed said. He began unzipping his pants.

Let's go to the city one day, Margie said. Before New Year's. Like Halloween. We can go to FAO Schwarz.

Ed's penis, by this point, was flopping in the cool air.

Sure, he said. Sure, anything you want. Come on.

Margie knelt down.

Do you promise? she said.

Yes, he said. Yes, yes!

All right, Margie said. I'll let you wait on it. This way you'll be sure to remember. And she walked away back toward Marine Park.

Ed Monahan picked himself up, and zipped up his jeans. He stood, breathing hard, under the tree for a minute, giving time to compose himself. Little shit, he said, under his breath, even though he knew that only crazy people talked to themselves. Little pussy shit, he thought in his head. Pinko-commie-liberal shit.

Ed fumed out of the nature center, crossed wide Avenue U, and continued into the parking lot. He went to his bike and started fumbling with the lock, until he realized that the motorcycle pack zipper had been jimmied. It was flapping open on one side. All his leftover string cream and plastic shooters were gone. Ed gargled a noise up in his throat. Who steals from a drug dealer? he wanted to know.

He looked around him. He squinted at the other people around the parking lot. There were the Caribbeans playing cricket. Dressed all in white, like cruise ship waiters. The fucks, he thought. They wouldn't dare. He looked at the people walking by on Avenue U. He looked at the do-rags hanging out of the back of their jeans. Ed's eyes narrowed. But what could he do? He got on his bike and rode away.

Coming around the oval, closer and closer to the flagpole, at the base of Marine Park, he approached the basketball courts, the perfect showcase ones that people were playing on, all hours. At the chain-link fence he paused and dismounted. Locked his bike up again.

Ed had always been a good basketball player; it was the only thing he had talent for. He'd been born, sometimes it seemed, dribbling. His daddy encouraged him. It's a white man's game, he'd say. Don't you forget that. And with the three-point line, who could say it wasn't? Ed was a born shooter.

At the Marine Park courts, he left his bike behind him, and walked out into the open, his jeans tight against his legs. Who's next? he asked a black man who was wiping sweat from his forehead with a rag.

———————

Ed found a good three, and they had next, and it was only two points left. He had a Hasid on his team, and the fat black man. It seemed like the team they were up against had been on court for days. One of them, in a Fordham jersey, dunked for the second-to-last point.

I'll take Fordham, Ed said, when they got on the court. The black man shrugged and fell in down low. The Hasid put a hand up to check his yarmulke, and took the man on the wing. Ed, who had the ball in his hands, was ready to check it. All right, Ponytail, let's do this, Fordham said. Just shut up, Ed said.

Fordham scored first, and he did it easily, juking left against Ed, and it was all Ed could do to stay on his feet. One, said Fordham. But then he passed it off to a teammate, who missed his shot. Ball, Ed called, from the top of the key, and the Hasid shrugged and gave it to him. He didn't have to think about it, he just caught and shot. He didn't have to look. He could hear the cleanness of the ball going through a rim with no net. Two, Ed said.

It's only one, Ponytail, Fordham said. We play by ones here.

Check, Ed said. Ball in, agreed Fordham. He checked in the ball. Ed passed it to the fat black man down low, who immediately passed it back. This time Ed didn't just shoot it—he waited until he could look Fordham in the eyes. Look at me, his eyes said. This is the beginning. And then he shot, one fluid motion. Three, Ed said. Nigger, can you count? Fordham asked.

Ed got the ball back. He scored twice more, and then Fordham started calling things.

Travel, he said. Ed had taken half a step and a dribble toward the wing. Get out, Ed said. Respect the call, said Fordham. Ball never lies. And he tapped the ball out of Ed's hand, took the test three, sunk it. Ed gave up possession.

The next one was carry. Carry, called Fordham. Man, get out of here, Ed said. Fordham just cocked his head to one side, until Ed passed him the ball for the ball-never-lies shot. He made it. Ed let him take it.

Then charge. All his years of street ball, nobody'd ever called a charge on him. He'd barely tapped Fordham on his way to the middle. Come on now, Ed shouted, let's be reasonable. His fat black teammate piped up, Yeah, come on now, that wasn't much of a charge. You fucking people, Ed continued, spitting. Hey now, the fat black man turned on him. What's all this? You people, Ed said again. You ruin everything. Can't play with you for nothing.

The Hasid had edged off the court.

Fordham was holding the ball dangerously against his hip.

I think you better leave now, Fordham said. You better get off my court.

Yeah, I'll head, Ed Monahan said. Just my kind of day, he said. He walked over to where he'd locked his bike up, but it was gone. Faggot, Fordham said from behind him.

It's not a long walk home for Ed from Marine Park to where he lives, south and east and close to the water. Along the way he thought about many things—people on welfare, stealing his money. Having kids at seventeen. Popping them out on the rest of us. He thought of his no-good girlfriend, Margie, and what little use she was to him. Just four days ago she'd spent the night, woke up with her naked body beside him, her hips touching his. But he slept with his jeans on. She woke up and took them off.

Ed unlocked the door to his house, locked it behind him. He had many locks, many latches, and he latched them all up. In his sink were the plates from his TV dinner the night before. He left them. He went into his bedroom and opened his phone.

Four rings. Margie didn't answer. He hung up before it could go to voice mail, sat down on the bed and called again. Four rings. She didn't pick up. Her recorded message came on, and Ed listened to her voice. He lay back on the bed, and let his boner rise against his jeans. He called her again, and listened to her voice. He rolled over on his side, reached for his bedside nightstand. He took out a condom and his daddy's gun.

Jeans off, he felt freer. His bedroom door was open, as if company might arrive. He eased the condom on, felt his back straighten in pleasure as it went all the way down. He held the gun in his left hand, his penis in his right. The gun was heavy, in his bad hand. He was, of course, right-handed. Sharp three-point shooter that he was, even the great Ed Monahan couldn't masturbate lefty.

There came a time when he fell back full against the bed. His right hand continued doing its business. The gun, in his other hand, lay flat against the mattress. He felt heavy, in a way he hadn't all day. He arched his back, searching for the space above him. When he came, he watched it happen, watched the condom's inside get painted white, watched it shrink and collapse. Vindicated, he let the gun slide to the floor. There was a low, warm light through the window. He didn't need Margie. He knew that now. It was silly of him to think otherwise. He didn't need anyone. He was enough. He could make a new world, just out of him, right here.

WE WERE SUPPOSED

We were supposed to go see a movie, get coffee, return calls, kiss, be alone, share a meal together, sleep on the same side of the bed, date, turn the radiator lower, find a studio, get two keys, move out for a while, get coffee, talk, see other people, get drunk, take a cab back to your place at two in the morning, fuck, return calls, date our friends, be angry, run six miles on the sidewalk, take a vacation, try again; get sunburned, sleep on the same side of the bed, reminisce, copyedit, get fired, find new jobs, move to San Francisco, eat only in Italian restaurants, get engaged, wear rings, wear black and console your mother, move back to Brooklyn, find an apartment, have your mother move in, be unhappy—paint the windowsills, drag your fingernails across the floorboard, over the socket with a dusting rag—be parents, buy diapers, find preschools with appropriate learning philosophies, read science books, play classical music, hire babysitters, write Christmas letters, go on family vacation (hate Disneyland, ride It's a Small World twice, because the kid loves it), go home, drive to rock concerts with your college friend Stanley, lock the bedroom door, go to Little League, scratch blood on our chests when the kid gets a concussion, play three-way catch, kick soccer balls, gain weight, go to funerals, move to Boston with the office, tell the kid he'll like the new school, buy a basketball hoop, be pulled from your mother in assisted living, drink two glasses of red wine at dinner, watch you drink no wine at dinner, stew, be bored in Boston—me walking alongside graveyards, discovering poetry cafés, coming home alone at four in the morning—drive the kid to school, take online classes, go on family vacation, have sex, write longer Christmas letters, watch a De Niro movie that hasn't been on in a while, buy a leather jacket and walk along the water, standing one foot leaned behind the other, watching people, watching men, tell the kid it's not about him; make money, go on family vacation, argue on the balcony while the kid texts, come back, reminisce, edit applications, share a meal, bring your mother home, take prom pictures, shake the kid's hand, bring the girlfriend on a weekend trip, feel the kid cry, explain love, put the kid's head on our chests like we used to put ours, unpack the car on a college campus, walk around with college sweatshirts, watch the kid not turn around, wait for the kid to call first: buy books we don't need any longer, pick grass stems by the river, press our names into each other's backs with our fingers sitting on a park bench, stand at a gas station and let the gas drip, go see a movie, get coffee, return, kiss, be alone.

PALMS

Amanda remembered her first palming like Martin's hand was still on her head; large, knuckly. Make you smart, Martin said. She submitted to it, even though she didn't like the feel. Her father, Rich, felt uncomfortable, but there were some things you had to do. He had been back in the house on a tentative basis, and his wife wouldn't want to hear he was making trouble in the neighborhood again, with Martin of all people. Martin was on the second stair of his stoop. We'll be going along now, Martin, Rich said. It's fine, Martin said. She'll be all right now. He removed his hand from her head. Now that Amanda was an adult he didn't give her palmings. The Braiker boy, though, who lived next door, still got them. He was in high school. He wondered if when he graduated he wouldn't. There was something comforting about Martin softly rubbing the top of his head, when he said hello. It might make him smart: who knew.

Nobody knew much about Martin other than that he sat on his stoop every morning, watching the B2s go back and forth, both directions. He never wore long pants, unless it was snowing out. He got a haircut every few weeks. Weekends he took a walk to Marine Park, biggest park in the borough other than Prospect, if you count that—but who does. He rollerbladed when he got there, a couple of times around. If he knew people that he passed, he gave them palmings, but only if he knew them. Some mothers pulled their youngest kids away, because it seemed odd. They moved to the bike path when they saw him coming, and put a hand up to wave, and he did the same. Otherwise he kept to himself, with large headphones on, listening to music low enough that no one else could hear.

There had been a piano teacher who rented the basement of Martin's house for many years, a middle-aged woman who'd been to conservatory in Russia. She kept a handwritten sign wedged under the knocker on the door saying "Piano Lessons," with her phone number. Amanda had been to her, even, though the Braiker boy was too young. People say Martin was friendly with the woman; that, when children showed up at the basement for their lessons, they sometimes saw Martin through the window sitting on the piano bench turning the sheet music pages. When she stood up to get the door she would pat his head, and answer the bell. Some lessons he sat there listening, for the first part at least, and then he would go out on his stoop. The woman, people said, wrote the word *practice*, in long loopy letters, on every page of their children's music books. She underlined it, many times, sometimes so hard that the page broke. She moved out after she hit one of her students. The boy had been playing a chord with the wrong final finger, over and over again—she lost it. Martin was the one who came to the door as the student burst through, face and eyes black and blue. Ever since then he was alone in the house and on the stoop, though the piano lessons sign stayed. It curled up from the humidity, blotched from raindrops but never totally ruined, protected by the eaves.

When Amanda moved back to the neighborhood a few years after college, after she'd lived in San Francisco for a while and felt it was time to go east, she decided not to go back home to her mother. Rich was out again at that point. There would have been plenty of room. But she had a good job for Pfizer, the drug company that she'd started working for in college. It wasn't that nobody had expected Amanda to go to college, but one of the city universities would have been fine, don't you think? her mother liked to say. She had always been the best basketball player in the neighborhood. They put her on the boys' B team once she started for Good Shepherd. And in high school she only got better, particularly after she hit her woman's height. Rutgers recruited her and gave her a scholarship, but not enough, of course, to pay for everything. Pfizer let her temp part-time in the off-season, at the office in Newark. The local EVP had played for St. Francis. When Amanda quit the team her sophomore year, they let her work as many hours as she could. She graduated, but it hadn't really mattered.

The house was ten blocks away from where she grew up. The B2 stopped right in front, on its way to Kings Highway, where Amanda got the Q to take her into the city, where she worked as a regional accounts manager. It was a good bus; it came on time; it was clean. Amanda could sit on it and work. She could sit out on her stoop and wait for it to arrive, no more than a minute or two. Some days, if she wasn't outside yet, the bus driver dawdled over someone's MetroCard. He had a soft spot for Amanda. She brought him a Christmas card with a Buckley's gift certificate every December. When she went up the bus steps Martin waved from his stoop.

It wasn't long before Amanda started seeing Robert Dillon, who was working at her office in Manhattan. He was an outside hire whose contract was with a PR firm, but he was working with the regional VP to rewrite the copy on the Pfizer website. They sat in the VP's corner office for hours while the VP brainstormed on and on about what Pfizer stood for, what communities they were looking to help and be a part of, what the essence of their business was. Robert took dutiful notes and asked pointed questions. Some of them verged on the very personal. Sometimes the VP would ask Robert for a line from literature that he could then riff off: *We beat on, boats against the current, medical advancements moving up.* Robert told Amanda this in her home. Soon Robert and Amanda were commuting together on the B2. The Pfizer contract was long-term and open.

Amanda's favorite time of the day was early morning, when she woke up without an alarm so as not to disturb Robert, and dressed silently in the running clothes she'd laid out for herself the night before—an old basketball T-shirt, formfitting nylon shorts. When she had lived in San Francisco, she would wake up early and run the hills above the Castro, where every once in a while she would get a peek at the water. It had seemed sunny then, even in winter. But back home in Marine Park, sometimes she'd start her run in the dark, and her route was dictated by which streetlamps would still be on, on the outer rim of the park. With the sun coming up behind her she raced her streetlamp shadow to the next light, until, on her third mile or so, the sun was up enough. Then she crossed Avenue U and went over to the salt marsh, where she could run by the water like she used to—except there were no hills here, none at all. This wasn't a problem for running, really. It had been for sledding when she was five, before basketball took over the winter. But now, grown up, hills seemed superfluous. On flat ground, she could run effortlessly and focus on nothingness; not pain in her legs, not the heavy pull of her breath; not her father. By the time she got back and was out of the shower Robert would just be stirring.

Robert had grown up in Brooklyn but not in Marine Park. He'd been to a liberal arts college where he studied literature and media, and his favorite bars were in the Village. He'd never met anyone quite like Martin, or when he thought carefully about it, he guessed he'd just never been in such close proximity to someone like him before. It's got nothing to do with Marine Park, Amanda said indignantly. The guy is touched as shit. But Martin had been around so long that the neighbors were superbly used to him by then, and that was a palpable feeling. Some evenings, when Amanda was in the shower or on business calls, Robert would sit outside with Martin. They'd each be on their own stoop, of course, the day stumbling to an end around them. Martin explained about palming once, but other than that he didn't have much to say. He said, It's how I stay warm inside. He wasn't embarrassed.

Can you try it on me? asked Robert then. Can I see what you mean? And so Martin stood up, and reached over the fencing separating the stoops, and put his hand down on Robert's head. Robert closed his eyes. Martin's hand reached in deep, through his thick hair, the tabs of all his fingers pulsing. Robert sat strangely like that, Martin's fingers moving above him. He waited for something to happen, for the message to hit him like experience, but it didn't. Robert thought that Martin seemed disappointed. Try me, Martin said, and sat down and took his headphones off. Robert extended his hand, but couldn't bring himself to touch Martin's head. He looked around him at the cold, quiet street. It's OK, he said. It is OK, said Martin. Martin put his headphones back on and listened to his music quietly.

The oldest Braiker boy was used to being on the rooftop. From there, either on his family's side or Martin's, he could see the long line of houses on R, and Fillmore and Quentin on either side. There was the large, imposing structure of PS 222, the local public school that he had gone to. When he was a student there he'd been convinced that the building had once been a rich man's mansion, and that's why the names of the rooms were so particular and color oriented. The Green Room, now the gym. The Blue Room, which still smelled like chlorine, on the first floor—now the cafeteria. The detail that clinched it was his discovery, in fifth grade, of a dumb-waiter, at the back of his fifth-floor classroom. He stuck his head inside during independent reading and the teacher ran over and held his legs while she screamed for the teacher's aid to go get help.

The rooftop was the only place where you could find flat open ground where nobody else was watching. The Braiker boy liked to lie there and imagine jumping from one plot of houses to another. They weren't all that far away, actually. The alleys were thin. Truth be told, he had measured the gap once and found that if he was an Olympic level long-jumper, on a practice jump even, he could do it. Sometimes he stood on the very edge, his sock-covered toes clinging to the siding. When the B2 came humming down the avenue it shook the houses a tiny, imperceptible amount, just enough that his body shivered a little. He was fairly certain he'd survive the fall. He'd heard of weirder things happening.

The Braiker boy had brought the Ventrone girl up to the roof with him. The morning of, he'd gone up and thrown some old blankets down. He didn't really think that anything would happen. They got on the bus to go to Madison HS together in the morning—both of their classes started on the early session. They didn't say anything about it, though they'd planned it off and on for a week. Second period, he could hardly listen to Mr. Kelly talk about unit circles and sine functions. When they got out, it was hardly noon. They stopped for pizza at Pronto's on R and Nostrand, sat in the new expanded section that looked like a real restaurant. The Braiker boy paid, which he hadn't done before. She said, All right then.

Her hand slipped on the ladder as she was going up. It was old and in his parents' closet. He'd pushed aside his father's pinstriped suits to give her room. The trapdoor was heavy, and he regretted having let her go up first, though he felt that this was the gentlemanly thing to do. From two rungs below he pushed with his hand as well. She was that much smaller than him. The grating sounded like something was broken. It happens all the time, he said. Once he'd gone up in a lightning storm and it had sounded much worse than that, the wetness of the metal and plaster hinge shrieking. He'd lain under an old rain jacket, looking below him at the double yellow line in the middle of the street, blinking from the rain.

With the Ventrone girl, there were no such weather issues. After looking over the edge, she ran up and down the block of houses, dodging the spaces where the trapdoors came up out of the roof. The Braiker boy, who had done this all before, sat down on the blanket. It was a wool blanket, and he regretted it suddenly. The Braiker boy picked up the blanket, smoothed it out, brushed the pebbles off the ground underneath it. When the Ventrone girl sat down with him he found that he had nothing to say except apologize for the rapid beating of his heart. His palms weren't sweaty. But he was sure that she could feel it.

Robert Dillon saw the Ventrone girl leave. He had the day off from work because the EVP was in Las Vegas for a conference. He was lounging in the living room reading a paperback by the wide front window when he saw her. He had almost been asleep. The lull of the B2s going by could do that. She stuck out, though, because she was walking so fast. She pulled the door shut too hard and walked toward Quentin with a purpose. Later, after Robert had cooked pasta for him and Amanda, after Amanda had finished her daily glass of wine, he laughingly told her about it. Amanda had just gotten off the phone with her father, who had moved back into the house, and Robert was casting around for things to say. Funny story, he said, today. Amanda was indignant. You saw that happening and you didn't say anything? They're underage; their parents should know. Robert was surprised. He didn't know whether to tell Amanda that he'd lost his virginity in his freshman year of high school, or whether it was too late. He tried to think of something else to talk about. I'm sure Martin saw too, he said.

Right, Amanda said. That's useful.

Amanda's father, Rich, wasn't all that bad a man. True, he was known by the neighbors to stomp out the front door, slamming hands on everything: not just the door, their car sometimes even, so that they wanted to bring it up, but who could have the heart. He was the football coach and assistant baseball coach at Madison. He'd been all-everything at Madison when he went there, in the seventies, lettering in football and baseball. Baseball had been his true love. He played football because it got you some respect. But he'd grown to like it as a coach. Had to—he didn't have any other options. There wasn't any way he was going to be a fireman, or a cop. He wasn't that stupid. The longtime field caretaker, Grady, retired his senior year, and they hired Rich for after he graduated. He was already working the day of. The principal said to him, Rich, you can get your robe later. First we need some more help with the bleachers. His mother never forgave him.

It got so bad one summer, when he'd been looking particularly boozy and blotchy for days, he told everyone that he had cancer. Not everyone at first; first just the men at the Mariners Inn. Which was the incredible thing about that place, that they kept it to themselves. Nobody liked to talk about things like that. But then he started saying it to everyone, whenever he could. You know Rich has cancer, Big Bailey's wife said to Big Bailey one day. I heard about that, he said. He was stopping people on street corners, telling them, reeking. What could you say?

When his wife let him back into the house, it was autumn. It would have been fall baseball season already. He'd missed summer football training, and you couldn't mess with a team once you'd missed summer training. He hadn't even had a landline at the hole he found in Howard Beach until he moved back in. But now it was baseball season, the high school kind. Madison had gotten to the city championship the year before, and everyone thought they should do it again. Technically, Rich was the pitching coach, not that he knew anything about pitching. He assumed they'd found a new assistant. Some recent graduate who didn't want to go into the fire department either. Fewer and fewer, it seemed to Rich, were going since 9/11. Rich didn't blame them. He remembered that morning, driving to the middle school to pick up Amanda. I can walk, Dad, she'd told him. He had opened the car door for her. Is there going to be a war? she'd asked him. He was looking down the boulevard on Quentin, watching what looked like smoke across the island. Shut up, he said. He didn't let her go outside to pick up the papers that had floated the ten miles from across the river. He didn't want her to have that memory. Rich was good for a while after that, but soon he stopped. Everyone talked about it as little as possible. It was already a long time ago.

One day, when he finally worked up the courage to go back to Madison to pick up his personals, he ended up walking down R. When he walked anywhere around Marine Park on what he called his constitutionals—They keep up my constitution, he said to his wife; Do some laundry, she said—he always walked down R. Even if he had to go out of his way to do it. It was the widest street, and it didn't have stores on it. All the houses were clean. There weren't any broken windows. There were always people sweeping in front of their steps. When he walked by Thirty-Eighth he noticed that Martin wasn't on his stoop. No sign of life in his daughter's house either. One of these days, he'd go inside.

At Madison the junior varsity was already on the turf field. The varsity wouldn't be out for another hour or so; the head coach liked it that way. Rich stood by the chain fence, and watched the middle infielders turning double plays. They were mostly bumbling, a little overweight, as junior varsity kids tended to be. A kid at third base had sweatpants on. One of the second basemen at least understood the footwork, and Rich focused entirely on him—the way you do when you're watching people dance, if someone puts a song from the jukebox on, if there's only one pretty girl in the room the entire night; the way you zero everything onto watching her. Most beautiful was the way the kid transferred ball from glove. He had good, quick hands. Rich recognized it. He'd probably start on varsity someday. It was only four years, high school, but it felt like a lifetime. You came in, you grew up, you played shortstop, you graduated.

That afternoon there was a freak storm in the middle of the day. It hadn't smelled like rain. If you're from Marine Park you can smell the weather coming in from the ocean, before it breaks up against the hot swell of city air. Even still, it caught everyone by surprise. Amanda and Robert were sitting in folding chairs in their backyard, listening to a Rutgers game on the radio. Amanda knew that Robert didn't like basketball, but they listened to it anyway. The old man who lived on the end was on his deck, in a folding chair, ensconced in hanging vines. The Braiker boy was on the roof, clutching a blue windbreaker that he didn't need yet, deciding whether to find the Ventrone girl. There wasn't much they could do. They could walk around the park. There was a place he knew, covered by weeping willows, where they could sit on the grass. But it was getting cold. Though he didn't expect the rain. Point is, they were all outside when the storm came rolling in.

The windbreaker, when it got torn out of the Braiker boy's hand, shot away from him toward the edge of the roof and then down, into the cavern of Avenue R, the space between the rows of houses on either side. Because of the way the air currents worked, a small vacuum effect exhibited itself, sucking the blue windbreaker up against the side of the Braiker house. It got stuck on a window, entirely covering it, so that if anyone else in the Braiker house had looked, the world outside would have been cloaked in blue. Finally one of the branches dislodged close enough to the window, and tore the jacket free. The wind-suck pulled the jacket down Avenue R, crackling as it went.

It was a sight to see that windbreaker, on its trip down the avenue. When the wind paused or circled, it would begin to fall, sometimes dropping almost all the way to the black slick pavement, but never landing, because the wind was strong enough to pick it up again. It scared the life out of the Chinese woman who collected recycled bottles, pushing her cruise-ship shopping cart of smudged and sticky multicolored plastic ahead of her. She would later, because of the incident, become far more religious than she had been. She would get all her bottles safely to where she lived, all the way down Quentin, in the basement of a house she rented from an Irish landlord, with her recently unemployed husband, who refused to work with his hands. She would believe in later days that it had been the blue flash that saved her, with the branches and leaves and house sidings falling around her. There were tornadoes in Queens, the nightly news said. They had news camera video of it, though it hadn't looked like what she'd thought tornadoes looked like—just a wide, dark skein of dirt, like it was a foggy day.

Rich stumbled back from Madison in the opposite direction of the wind. He had somebody's old varsity jacket in front of him, which he'd grabbed off the side of the fence when the team ran from the field. Two jokers tried to stay and hit each other fungoes, and no one had told them to stop, because the coaches were inside. They left when the wind began batting the ball to the ground. But Rich had already started for home. The varsity jacket smelled warm and sunny, like a piece of clothing left in the back of a pickup truck for too long, on a road trip down to Florida.

Martin was on the stoop when Rich got to Avenue R. Rich had started to jog back on Quentin, slow shuffling steps he hadn't remembered he could do. Rich paused for just a second across from Martin, and yelled hysterically for him to get out of the weather. With the wind and the leaves flying and the branches coming down, it seemed a moment fit for hysteria. Rich relished it, relished the yelling. He was happy to be appropriately excitable. Martin was cowering under some sort of jacket himself. It wasn't like he was sitting there watching the rain. He didn't have his headphones with him. Though it was barely raining at that point. Rich yelled again, more hysterical even, for Martin to get himself inside. Martin was answering, but Rich couldn't hear him, and the wind was getting even higher. Rich turned around to watch Martin as he stumbled away, but Martin didn't make any motions to get up. He walked like this, waiting for Martin to do something, until he walked into a tree, and then he turned around and ran until his wife let him back in the house.

No one really agrees how it happened. The number of stories after, you'd think everyone was watching at their windows, but how many of them could that have been? How many people actually saw Martin run into the middle of the street? Was it because the wind ripped the piano lessons sign out from the door-knocker and he was trying to get it? Did he see someone or something through the rain? It was a Sunday: he could have been planning on going to the park to rollerblade. Nobody knows. When he went into the street, in the middle, the branches falling around him, it looked through the windows like he was screaming, but how could you hear something like that? Then the rain started coming down in sheets. The fire trucks got there first. They'd been trained in emergency response to make up for cost-cutting in ambulance service. The three firemen carried him from the street into the fire truck, his body flailing wildly. His tongue was in the middle of his teeth and his arms jerking all around him. The driver put on the siren. No one went away from their windows.

The cleanup, when it happened, didn't take long. It's surprising how things get back to normal. Everyone wondered where Martin had got to. Four weeks later there was a FOR SALE sign up on his door. Dead, the Braiker boy heard. Hospitalized, Amanda said to the Ventrone girl waiting for the B2 bus one morning. Don't be stupid, Rich told people at the Mariners, drinking his lemonade and coffee. He moved to a condo on Kimball Street. You'd think it was a ghost story. The new inhabitants of Martin's house didn't sit on the stoop. Their children, like all children forever in Marine Park, had garage sales out there in the fall. They sat in front of the old books and toys and clothing in their brightly colored uniforms. They never got palmings, but they grew up anyway.

*O*ne fall day we sat on the stoop in front of our house, waiting for people to come buy from our garage sale. It's not a garage sale, said Lorris. It's a stoop sale. But that doesn't sound as good, I said. A step sale then, he said. Fine, I said, a step sale. In the crevice from the sidewalk and the indentation that the bus made coming through every morning, there was a puddle of water, a quarter foot deep and buzzing with gnats. Lorris was picking up brick pebbles from our neighbor's unswept stoop and landing them in the puddle.

An old woman stopped and asked how much the paperbacks were.

We're selling them for one dollar, I said.

One dollar! That's not enough, she said. I'll give you three.

Told you, Lorris said to me.

The woman smiled fondly at Lorris. Do you like to read? she said.

Yes, said Lorris.

What's your favorite book? she said.

His head dipped down and he became less excited. He hated questions about favorites: red versus blue, Yankees or Mets, the sport that he was best at. He didn't like making choices.

He's reading Sherlock Holmes now, I said.

The old woman patted his arm and he looked carefully at her sandals.

Can you tell me the plot from one of your favorite Sherlock Holmes stories? she asked.

Lorris's face looked like when you press pause in a video game.

I'll give you an extra dollar, she said.

We'd only made six dollars all morning.

How about if your brother helps you? she said. He still looked the same way. Or any story at all. Otherwise I'm leaving. She mimed walking away.

Lorris took his hands out of his pockets and put them on my arm, like someone had pressed start.

Tell her a story about us, he said.

ATTACHED

orris asked if he could get a ride home from the train station later that night somewhere in the neighborhood of three a.m. It was a Friday in December, and I hadn't left the house in a week and a half, which is what happens when you live at home. I said, What, you don't think I got plans of my own? He just stood there looking in the mirror in the living room adjusting the hat he'd borrowed from me and never returned, a little to the left, more to the right, until he got the perfect tilt he was after the whole time. It was a flat-brim, the first one I'd ever gotten, gray with the Mets logo in front. I'd never liked the color royal blue, and that's what all the other Mets caps were. But this one I'd connected with, and I used to wear it everywhere, until Lorris started asking for it and I gave it to him one birthday. People are always giving people useless things for birthdays. That's something I can't abide with.

He said, And it might be closer to four—I'm not really sure. I said, How about you give me a call and we'll see where I'm at, and if I'm in any state to drive. Really, I meant if I was awake. He said that sounded fine, and asked if I minded if he took some of the cologne Mom had gotten me for Christmas. It had a note on it that said, *Something nice for someone nice.* I told him it was in my junk drawer, which I hadn't opened in a while, but it was somewhere in there, if he wanted to dig into it and look.

Nights I drove around. I had a 1991 Ford Taurus that my aunt had gotten rid of when she got a new job. She didn't want to own a car that was practically twenty years old. She'd been working with Bank of America and then there was what she said they called the Little Slowdown, and she'd been out of work. Another place hired her a year later, with pay cut and demotion, but she took it, because it wasn't so easy to get jobs anymore.

It was a dirty tan car, and whenever I drove my mother to the Key Food to get groceries, she insisted we stop at the gas station and fill up the tank. I wasn't making much of an income. I worked at the cell phone place at Kings Plaza a couple days a week. That's all the time they could give me, though they said they wished it could be more. I was good with following directions, went along with the company policy of introducing yourself and asking the customer's name when they got in the store. I liked hearing the names, trying to guess what block they lived on, if they were on the right side or the left side of Flatbush. I wasn't taking any classes that year. Sometimes these things just happen.

When we hadn't gone to the grocery store in a little while or I didn't have any extra to put in the tank, I walked around. There's a painting-poster my dad has, on the wall leading up to our bedrooms, of a café somewhere with people sitting in it, the sky dark at the top and the only light coming from inside the café. He said it was Barcelona, but he'd never been. Why don't you go there and talk to someone, if you're so attached to it? he said. It's not like Marine Park had that, though it wasn't so bad. I could stand for hours looking at the Lott House, the old Dutch estate between Fillmore and S, the one that was Parks Department property and that the Brooklyn College archaeologists were doing excavations on, to find old slave quarters. I'd been on the porch once, when they decorated for Christmas. Every night, they put a candle in the top middle window, and I liked leaning on the fence looking at that and the old wood. The windows were shuttered up, and there were signs to stay off the grounds around the house. They thought the ground was unstable, because there were supposed to be Underground Railroad tunnels underneath. This had been one of the last stops. They'd get them out at night somewhere through a false plank in the kitchen floor.

Lorris texted the first time at midnight, said, *Place is lame, but somewhere else soon. Also, you could come, call if you want to.* He always wrote in full sentences in texts. Some girl had berated him about it once, he said. She said, You're going to Williams next year and you write like this? At first he just did it for her, but then it was easier to be right for everyone.

I was still in front of the TV at home. Mom was sitting in the kitchen, ice on her legs for the shin splints, massaging her feet. A few hours before Dad had said he was going out for a movie. Do you want to go? he asked Mom aggressively. Does it look like it? she said, pointing at her feet. She'd had the ice on since she got back from work. I told her, Mom, maybe take a day off from running once or twice, and they might feel better. She's like, I'm a school secretary. I sit at a desk all day long. You ever see a school secretary take a lunch break? she says. I have to move around a little or I'll forget how. She's scared that she'll get Alzheimer's like her mother did.

I texted Lorris back that it was nice of him, but I was a little busy at the moment. Didn't want to make something up, because you could always tell—the name of such and such club, friends that didn't live here anymore. Too easy to say too much and get caught in the lie. That would have been the embarrassing part. He couldn't even drive yet. I said, *Let me know when you do need the ride, I'll probably be OK to come get you.*

We live in the worst possible place for getting anywhere. It's a twenty-five-minute walk to the subway, or a bus, the least-served area by the MTA in the whole goddamn city. I checked on a map one day. My dad always complains about the fact that Mom moved him into a two-fare zone. He means that you have to pay twice, once for the bus and once for the Q train, if you're trying to get yourself into Manhattan, or even downtown Brooklyn, where everything that's happening is. I'm pretty sure he knows that it's all one fare today, even if you have to transfer, but he's been driving so long now and takes trains so infrequently that you never know. He got mugged too many times in the eighties, even when he was on dates. That's the kind of embarrassing thing that'd drive a guy to the DMV, no problem.

At one thirty I turned off the third straight *Law & Order* and went through the kitchen out the back, past Mom, who had fallen asleep across three chairs. I could've woken her, but I don't think she really sleeps soundly until she hears Lorris back in the house. She'd go up and pretend to be in bed before we got back. I pulled out of the alleyway, quietly, then turned the music up higher. It's a five-minute drive to the station at Kings Highway, and at this time of night I found a spot half a block from the entrance. I shut the car off and waited.

The only time I ever remember going into the city all together by train was when we did family outings to the Met. When we were little we used to do it once a year, in the summer, at that point in July when me and Lorris were too jumpy with being out of school and Mom was tired of babysitting us. Then Dad would take a day off from work at the driver's ed place and we'd all get on the B2 bus to Kings Highway. When Dad took a day off he didn't want to drive, period. So we did it the whole way, public transportation, as if we didn't have a car.

Kings Highway, where we get the train, is the best station in the city. In the winter, it looks like one of those old Russian train stops where you can imagine people escaping wars. People with all sorts of weird belongings in canvas bags, with their babushka scarves, huddled together against the cold. At nighttime, you could see the trains far out in both directions, a B stretching in from Coney Island, doors open and the smell of the sand, or a Q coming down from the city, off the Manhattan Bridge. When you catch the Q you have to know to sit on the bench on the right side; I mean the side on your right when the Q is heading toward Manhattan. Then you're in a perfect position when it goes over the river to see all the skyline through the Brooklyn Bridge. I can't understand people who sit on the other side, looking at nothing. It's like they *don't* ride the train every day.

We couldn't go into the Met without playing in the Ancient Playground first. It was right next to the museum, with pyramids and stone temples that you could climb up, ladders on the inside. Lorris and I would time each other in a circuit down and through the tunnels. Mom and Dad sat on the street end, watching the cars and not really talking. When we had our half hour we went inside, and Dad would put four quarters down for all of us. No one was dumb enough to give him a look, but he always said he was ready for it. *The point is it's free*, he liked to say. *It's for the people. I used to leave a nickel.* I liked the part with the colonial rooms that are made just the way they used to look. God, I could look at those forever. And the big glass room with the fountain and Greek sculptures.

There's one of two bears that's smooth and looks out of place; that was Lorris's favorite, but the rest are mostly people, caught in uncomfortable positions.

Few months before, I'd gone to the Met with some girl from the neighborhood. She was studying art at New Paltz. I hadn't seen her in a while and I figured I'd give her a call. She said the Met was a great idea; it was like her favorite museum ever. I picked her up in Sheepshead, and we drove in. Let me tell you, it was a good idea to go to the Met with her. She took me into rooms I didn't even know they had there. And she always knew something about what we were looking at, especially the Greek pottery, which was her specialty. When we got to the colonial rooms, she asked if I knew that most of the fireplaces came from real houses here in New York City. They packed up whole walls and trucked them over, she said, her brown hair shaking as her eyes got bigger. I said I hadn't known about that, even though of course I did, because I thought it was making her feel good to tell me things. I think it worked.

In front of the French impressionists, I had my thumb in my pocket, and she slid her hand around the little hole my arms made. "See when you step back," she said, pointing, "it comes into even clearer focus. You have to look at a painting from different sides. Once I saw the Gertsch painting of the girl, and her eyes follow you when you change sides." She had a poster of it up in her room; she showed me later that night. When she was in the bathroom after, I tried it, going from one side to the other, and the eyes followed sure, but even better was that the expression in her mouth changed. Pouting and sensual on one side and depressed on the other. The whole rest of the time in the museum she kept her hand around my arm there.

Lorris texted at three to say he was on his way: *Is it all right if we drop off a few of my friends on the way home? Guys from the baseball team.* I said, *Yeah, I might be a little late, but meet me a block up from the station.* I had the key in the ignition so I could listen to the radio but save the gas. You'd be surprised how much time you can waste just going through stations looking for a good song. When trains came in I turned it off and opened the windows so I could listen to everyone going by—which is what I imagine Barcelona in that painting Dad has would be like, sort of late at night but people still all around, taxis off the avenue. The taxis in Marine Park were all manned by Russian immigrants, most of whom didn't know English. They played cards in the control center right next to the station, where you could go to pick up a ride. Nights I wasn't driving—if I came back late from an outing when my boys were back from college, or hanging out after work—sometimes I got one of them to drive me back, if I couldn't stand the idea of the walk. Sometimes you could converse, if you had the right charades aptitude, and if so they'd give you a swig from the warm vodka they had in paper bags in the glove compartment. You'd offer it back to them, they'd make a fake show of looking around in the empty streets, and then laugh that big hairy laugh and have a drink and an indistinguishable toast with you.

When his train came it was crowded, and he came out of the green station doors in a cluster of his friends. They were all just graduating that year, nothing they were supposed to be doing. It wasn't like they only did this on Fridays. Every other weekday too, Lorris'd be creeping back at three or four in the morning. I didn't really mind when he asked me for a ride; it was better than waiting at home trying to stay awake longer than he was.

He opened the front door and he was still wearing my goddamn hat, the gray Mets one. He said, Hey, and put on his seat belt while his friends opened the back doors. I looked through the rearview mirror at them, all steaming from the cold even though no one had jackets on. When they closed the doors the windows immediately began to steam up. I said, Where's all the girls? and they started roaring, and that made me feel good.

How was your night? he said.

Good, I said.

Someone stole our jackets at the warehouse.

Always happens, I said. I told you not to take one.

Yeah, well, he said.

You're just lucky it's not the hat.

He took it off and held the flat brim between his fingers. He traced the NY, which popped up off the front. I know, he said.

We dropped everyone off, the hand slaps at the stoops, the car doors open and shut. The impossibility of red lights at that time of night, just look around in all directions and make sure no cops or other cars were around, and go. Treat everything like a stop sign. I knew where all the cameras were in this neighborhood, had known since I was as old as Lorris is. He never paid attention when we drove anywhere, had his eyes on his hands.

His friend Omar was last, second base to his shortstop, and they promised to see each other tomorrow. It was a few blocks from our house, and once Omar got to the door I went to put the car in drive, but Lorris put his hand on top. Let's make sure he gets in OK, he said. We watched the living room light go on, and then go off, and then an upstairs bedroom one flicker quietly. You know we can go now, Lorris said.

I checked my mirrors and there was no one and we pulled away. When I first got my license and would drive with Lorris, we used to circle the block if a good song was on the radio and we didn't want it to end. Then in the alley, he'd hop out and open the gate, and I'd pull in slowly, avoiding the garbage cans, trying to get the car in as straight as our dad does.

Where are you going? Lorris said.

Let's drive a little, I said.

It was only a few blocks to the old house, the farmhouse. We used to think it was haunted. I pulled in front by the white fence. It's funny, even in a neighborhood with so few parking spots, no one parks in front of the Lott House. Lorris gets out first like it was his idea, and he hops the fence, smoothly, two hands and a leg leap, and he leans up against the big tree next to its wide porch, a weeping reacher like I've only seen pictures of, except for here.

By the time I get there he's pulled a lighter out of his pocket, and a joint, already rolled. Omar had to get rid of it, he says.

I didn't know you smoked, I said.

I don't, he said. I just tried it once last week. I don't think it does anything for me, though.

You're probably right, I say.

He lights it, and passes it to me. I take a nice small puff, like I always do, and he takes it back, does the same thing. He holds it between his fingers for a second. Do you want this? he asks. When I shrug he sticks it in a cluster of dirt and grass next to the tree.

There are a few wood steps up to the front door, and we stand there, watching the street. A Chevy Malibu goes by but it doesn't notice us.

You thinking about finishing at Brooklyn this year? he asks.

Maybe, I say, maybe.

I know some kids who took a while there because they were working, he says. He looks at his legs.

It's all right, Lorris, I say.

I think about how infrequently you say someone's name out

loud. I mean someone close to you, like a good friend or a brother. That girl from the Met, I think I might have said her name once. Leila, I said. Why didn't you call? she said.

I put a finger diagonal across my mouth and take the four steps left to the door. Lean my shoulder into it hard and the lock just clicks. I pull my cell phone out of my pocket, open it up to use the light.

Later, back in the car, we listen to one song before heading home. I don't even remember what it was. They played a lot of Michael Jackson that summer, it could have been him. Lorris and I had always liked his high voice, his style. Neither of our voices ever dropped much.

In the alleyway, the red bike was locked up against the fence, telling us that our father was home. He liked to bike to the movies, liked the ride back. It meant longer on his own time. It was only out in Sheepshead Bay, and he rode home along the water. When we closed the gate behind us, I saw the bathroom light go on, our mother doing recon. When we walked in, she'd be quiet as anything, like she'd been asleep since spring.

When they brought Lorris home from the hospital when he was born they gave me a toy cement mixer truck. I wanted to drive construction back then. I don't remember but they said they did it so I wouldn't be upset. I remember that I never used to be that attached to anything. Once we were playing cowboys and Indians and I shot a bow and arrow into his chest and he cried, but I didn't feel it. Hurts, he said over and over. There was a circle mark in the center from the plastic suction arrow tip. I'd licked it before pulling the string back to see if it would stick.

There was nothing much in the Lott House. I was expecting a room somewhere, all decorated like the ancestors were about to return. Period pieces of furniture and a table set with wood forks. Some gaping hole in the floor where the tunnels were, tunnels that we could jump into and wander the underground borough by night, dust flecks falling from the side walls where our wide arms trailed for balance. There were just fold-up chairs from Parks Department events. I guess there was nowhere else to put them. I pulled one out and kicked it open, slid it across the tile floor to Lorris, kicked one open for myself. For a minute he let us sit there. You OK? he said. Yeah, I said. Yeah, absolutely. Do you mind if we go now? he asked. He looked like he wasn't sure. I wanted to say how much I liked this place. I liked the way the wood felt under my feet. While I put the chairs back in the rack Lorris went out and waited for me by the car.

CAR PARKED ON QUENTIN,
BEING WASHED

On the morning of the funeral Lorris slept until his father woke him. Mr. Favero had woken earliest, so he went in the shower first. He shaved and came out. Wake up the boys, Mrs. Favero whispered, while she took off her faded T-shirt and bra. Mr. Favero didn't look at her bare back, although some mornings he did. She stepped into the shower. Mr. Favero walked into Jamison's room, where they were both sleeping in the air-conditioning, and put a hand on each of their heads.

Lorris had come home from college the day before. He was only staying for the weekend. Mr. Favero had waited on Thirty-Fourth Street, off Seventh Avenue, watching for the Megabus to come in. Then he and Lorris had left the car parked and walked into a corner coffee shop. Lorris bought his father a cup and a croissant, with a five from his wallet. Lorris drank a cup of tea himself, something Mr. Favero had never seen him do before. It was a dark little room, empty except for people using the bathroom before getting on a bus, or passengers carrying heavy bags looking for a bottle of water or directions afterward. The two of them sat at a window table and watched the charter buses slowly empty and leave. Mr. Favero asked questions, informed by their phone conversations, about school. When the coffee was gone they went outside to drive back to Brooklyn.

The room, facing the avenue, was quiet in the morning. Jamison woke first, although Lorris had been up and down before. He wasn't used to sleeping at home again. He always took some days to get accustomed to new beds, the new sounds of people breathing, the walls and creaking pipes. It had taken him a long time to fall asleep with his brother's breathing. Sleep OK? said Mr. Favero. The pullout bed was close enough to the real bed that he could lean in between both of them. Lorris nodded, and Jamison groaned. He rolled over and reached to the nightstand for the clock.

Mrs. Favero was the last one to get dressed. She had spent a long time picking between the dark navies and black blouses that she had in the closet. Mr. Favero was already downstairs, in a suit, looking at his watch and drinking coffee with the boys. Each of them took a mug. We should leave, Mr. Favero yelled up. You wait a minute, Mrs. Favero answered. She was talking to herself in the mirror.

The whole avenue was blocked off. There hadn't been any notices, nothing hung on trees or bus stop poles, but everyone had known to park their cars on the side streets. Mr. Favero led them off to where the car was on Kimball, reached around and opened the passenger-side door. Lorris and Jamison squeezed their legs into the back. Jamison fingered the broken handhold above his head. We need gas, said Mr. Favero. We're fine, Mrs. Favero said. There were other people getting into their cars on the side streets. Mr. Favero stopped at the stop sign. The Dentons' house next door to them was empty and quiet, and there were flowers on the sidewalk.

It was difficult to find a parking spot. Mr. Favero circled the church lot twice. Lorris remembered having youth baseball awards nights here, all the kids from the different teams in their different colors. Lorris's favorite had been yellow, the one year when they let him pitch. He'd been on the youngest Denton's team that year; they'd both played outfield together. They'd been in the same school until ninth grade, though now they weren't close. As they passed the entrance to the church hopelessly for a third time, Lorris was struck suddenly by the memory of one of those awards ceremonies, early in the summer, a lazy blue tinge to the night. Four ice cream trucks had been double-parked on the street fighting for customers. Someone finally came out of the gates to tell them to turn the jingles off. You couldn't hear the league commissioner, who was also a fireman and lived on Thirty-Sixth. Lorris had gotten the Most Improved Award, he remembered, and Tyler Denton had been MVP. Tyler was playing in college, though Lorris wasn't. For God's sake, Mrs. Favero said. I'll try Avenue V, said Mr. Favero. As they passed Avenue R and the front of the church they saw the long line of firemen walking slowly in through the front doors. They all had their dress uniforms on, like a September 11 memorial, year after year, the tenth anniversary just like the fifth. Lorris barely remembered it, though he was old enough to. He and Jamison had slept in the same room for weeks. The firemen walked down the double yellow line, in the middle of the closed street.

Good Shepherd was not a big church, though it wasn't a small one. It wasn't particularly well decorated. There was a large skylight stained-glass window up over the altar, which was supposed to be the crowning work of art, but looked strangely geometrical and out of place, almost like an Islamic mosaic. Mrs. Favero had once felt strongly that the boys go to church. Her mother had been like that. But it began to feel less and less important. Just the year before one of the deacons was accused of improper sexual conduct. I knew it,

Lorris had crowed, over the phone. He had already been at college. He always used to look at me funny, Lorris said. Mr. Favero had put an end to such jokes quickly. Enough, he said. The small bronze font for holy water at the front of the church was almost empty, and the ground was squeaky and damp around it, when the Faveros crossed themselves. They sat in the back row, because it had been so difficult parking. Lorris had only seen a coffin once before. The new priest, from some foreign country, stood up.

Later, at the house next door, everyone said what a nice service it had been. Genine Denton, the wife, was nodding quickly, her chin jutting out too far. People had said such nice things, Lorris heard someone say. He heard someone say, almost excitedly, *I* didn't know he went to Midwood! I didn't even know Midwood *existed* back then. The Stanton family was all there, showing the new family the ropes. No one played whiffleball on the corner of Thirty-Fourth and R, where the green sign was, the Fire Captain Thomas J. Stanton memorial corner. *I* didn't know his firehouse had been so close to the World Trade Center, a woman near Lorris gasped. The closest one, someone else answered. Make it through that and then. Lorris shook Tyler Denton's hand, but Tyler walked away before he could say much. Eventually Mrs. Denton went with Mrs. Favero next door, where they put the food that wouldn't fit in their fridge into the Faveros'. Then she sat on the couch next to Mrs. Favero. They talked about when their children used to play in the living room there. Mrs. Favero asked if she remembered Legos. Mrs. Denton said that she did. Mr. Favero came in the door with his hands in his pockets looking for them. He stood in front of the couch. He suddenly didn't know what to do.

That night, after they'd changed out of their good clothes, the ones they'd had in closets in plastic bags, they sat down to watch television. Mr. Favero had been on the couch there since dinner.

He hadn't done the dishes. There wasn't enough room for all of them on the couch, so Jamison lay on his stomach on the floor. He was laughing at the sitcoms. After the news, Mrs. Favero asked the boys to take the recycling out. Jamison looked at her strangely. Dad always takes the recycling out, he said. He was leaning up on his elbows. You could do something around here sometime, she snapped. Jamison got up and Lorris went with him.

They lugged the white bags out of the trash cans, in the backyard, dragged them around the alleyway and out to the front. Lorris noticed that the tree, in the backyard, looked even more like a face than it usually did—like one of those children's movies where inanimate objects come alive.

Check out the tree, Lorris said, while they passed it. The face.

Jamison looked at it. I never notice it, he said.

They put the recycling where it belonged, matching the rest of the white bags in front of the other houses. Lorris watched the grease from the tomato cans color the bottom of his bag. He thought about how long it would take to pool through the bottom. Jamison took out his cell phone, wiped his hands on his pants before touching the screen.

Who's that? Lorris asked.

A girl, Jamison said.

You're so full of it, Lorris said. You make it like it's a different girl every day. Show me the text.

I'm not showing you anything.

Here, Lorris said, and reached for the phone. Jamison jerked it away, finished the text, and put it back in his pocket. Give it up, Jamison said. He started walking up the stairs to the house. When he got to the top of the stairs he said, Maybe we can play some baseball this weekend, before you leave. He looked back at Lorris like he was waiting for an answer, so Lorris said, Course. Jamison went in and the door banged. It made Lorris feel good. Jamison was back and forth like that all the time. While Jamison went in, Lorris saw an upstairs light go off in the Dentons' house.

It was still light out, and warm. It would almost be summer. Lorris checked to see if the screen door stayed unlocked and walked up Avenue R, toward Flatbush. He didn't even have a sweatshirt on. There were no spaces between the houses here, as there weren't until right by Flatbush, after which they changed back again. They grew into each other on both sides. Most of them were painted red. Lorris wondered if someone had planned the houses out beforehand, or if they shot up in perfect rows. Suddenly he felt claustrophobic, the way he sometimes did on bus rides, when the ride was too long and it was already dark outside the window. There would be the cars flashing by on the other side of the highway, sometimes a gas station and lit-up rest stops, but that was it. The emptiness made him feel restless. That's how his legs felt, like even if he wanted to he couldn't get up. Tomorrow he would take the bus back to college.

On Quentin Road, in front of the supermarket, Lorris leaned back against a fire hydrant. A man on the same side of the street was washing his car. He was scrubbing with a thick sponge. Lorris watched him twist the material in his hand. There was a bucket of water on the ground next to him, the water sloshing against the edges. The hose next to the sidewalk was leaking and getting Lorris's shoes wet. The man worked over the same point on the car for a long time, and then he leaned his forehead on the hood and kept pressing, not looking. The metal at the top of the fire hydrant was biting into Lorris's leg, but he felt that it would be the most impossible thing in the world for him to leave just then.

THE TREE

We were heading out to buy a Christmas tree off Knapp Street. I thought we used to go to Marine Park, Lorris said. Tuh, said our mother. We never went there, she said. We haven't been there in years, she amended—They're too expensive. I thought I remembered always going to Marine Park to get our Christmas tree when we were kids, even after—sawdust on the ground, a pile of old cut-up trees in the corner of the parking lot, which would stay there until spring, when the Parks Department trucked them away: same weekend they dragged the baseball fields—but I guess I was wrong. My mother, a school secretary, is nothing if not together. Since Lorris has been in college she's been substituting in math. I'm in the basement, which has its own bathroom, just for a while. My father just kept driving. Is this Katy Perry? he asked Z100.

Avenue R forks like an ornament hook, and we went left onto Gerritsen. You follow that far enough, you get to the end of the world, where Brooklyn drops into the water, where the houses are small and waterproof. We used to play baseball there, Lorris and me, in socks too big for our feet. Across the street from the diamond is the library, where I went a few days ago, sick of nostalgia. Lorris and I had driven over together, talking about our problems.

He had become too introspective, in my opinion. Enough *thinking* about what was wrong. Just *do* something instead. Lorris nodded like he tends to, but I don't think he was satisfied. You can't make someone be satisfied by telling them.

The tree was easy this year. They didn't have many left. Got any Fraser firs? our mother asked. We always buy Fraser firs, she confided to the tree attendant in an elf hat. Good trees, he said, the felt ears jangling. Every year, she said. What about this little one? my father said, pointing at a Charlie Brown–size one. It was small and squat, wilting in the warm, unseasonable weather.

We got the tree tied on top of the van, this old green minivan we've had for a long time, and we started driving back. It was all easier than one time I remember—Seven years ago, my mother said. Maybe ten, she added—it was one of those two. That year, we got to Knapp Street and had the tree on top but couldn't make the car start. We called Triple A. Meanwhile, a blizzard started. Soon the snow was up to our ankles, and we were getting cold, and Triple A wasn't coming. I remember walking back to the house, all four of us with our hats and gloves on, looking like a ridiculous collection of amateur snowmen. Avenue R was disappearing beneath our boots. The news said things were happening elsewhere, but we couldn't tell. I almost didn't recognize the house until it was upon us, strange and framed by snowdrifts, crowded in by all the other homes. The Christmas lights were on in the window but there was an empty space in the center, for where we would put the tree.

ACKNOWLEDGMENTS

Thanks to Amy Hempel, who is a force of nature. Thanks to the incredible Bret Johnston and the Harvard English Department. Thanks to Jackie Ko, for expert guidance from beginning to end in addition to unflappable, undying support, along with Diego Núñez and everyone at Wylie. Thanks to Allison Lorentzen, who made this book better than it deserves to be and who knows what you see through the window on the Q, and thanks to Nick Bromley and copy editor Ryan Sullivan and everyone at Penguin. The story "Shatter the Trees and Blow Them Away" owes much to Richard Rhodes's remarkable *The Making of the Atomic Bomb*. Thanks to Andrew Miller and Jenny Jackson, Caroline Bleeke, Sofia Groopman, and Christina Thompson. To the Whelehans. To Emily Moore and the Byrnes family. Thanks to Charlotte Alter, for reading first and last and everything else. Most of all, for my family—my grandparents; aunts and uncles; my parents, Mary and Ken Chiusano; and my brother, Scott Chiusano. Who else to write for but them.